WELCOME TO CLARENCE BAY!

Winter in Canada. The words conjure up images of snow-covered ski hills, tobogganing with the children, hopping on the Skidoo and going for a wild ride over the frozen ice. But, inevitably, out come the dreaded snow shovels. Ugh! Many Canadians would rather share the indoor joys of the season with family and friends around the table or in front of the skating events on TV. Me? I love the ice dancing.

Winter in the small town of Clarence Bay is a lean and quiet time. The tourists have migrated back to the city and businesses are on short hours or shuttered for the winter. The days are shorter, cloudier, snowier. All the more reason to settle into a comfy chair by a warm fire, bring out the books or handicrafts, and renew the relationships lost in the hustle of summer.

Stormy Wedding is the third book in the Clarence Bay Chronicles: An ice storm has shut down the province but there's a wedding in four days. Can the groom Jesper and four friends save the day for the beloved bride LeeAnn? And what sort of mischief will the Christmas Spirit get up to?

Next up... *The Gossiping Detective*. Melody, of the infamous Gossiping Grishams and author of the Hatch, Match, and Dispatch column of the *Clarence Bay Beacon* is determined to become a real journalist. An unusual death occurs in town which might grant her that opportunity. Will police detective Gareth be a help or a hindrance?

There's more to come from Clarence Bay. So stay tuned!

I love to hear from my readers. Connect with me on my website at www.joanleacott.ca or Facebook, Goodreads and BookBub.

Come meet the neighbours and find new friends in Clarence Bay!

Joan Leacott

Stormy WEDDING

Clarence Bay Chronicles
Book 3

JOAN LEACOTT

WOVEN RED PRODUCTIONS
Toronto, Canada

Cover and Interior Design by Woven Red Author Services, www.WovenRed.ca
Edited by Brenda Chin, www.brendachin.com
Stock imagery is acquired under valid Standard Licences from Depositphotos Inc. and Adobe Stock via on-demand contracts. Fonts are acquired through valid licences with various vendors.

Stormy Wedding/Joan Leacott—1st edition, November 2023
ISBN ebook: 978-1-9994791-5-2
ISBN paperback: 978-1-9994791-6-9
ISBN large print hardback: 978-1-9994791-7-6

Many thanks to

my awesome friend and beta reader
Gina Grant

and my fabulous editor
Brenda Chin

and my generous piano teacher
Ann Edwards

and to the linemen, unsung heroes
who keep our world bright and warm.

These stories wouldn't be what they are without you.

Dedicated to...

My beloved Victor

and my wonderful sister Eileen.

Life wouldn't be the same without you.

FROZEN FLOWERS

Stormy Wedding 1

Four Days Before the Wedding

Shelby Hadley tipped the last of her beer into Denis's glass and leaned back in her chair at the Compass, Clarence Bay's favourite tavern for beer, burgers, and bands. Talking to a friend on his other side, Denis didn't notice her contribution to his drink. It kinda irritated her, though she couldn't say why. They'd been friends ever since either could remember. At one point, they could finish each other's sentences.

Not anymore.

Not since she'd left Clarence Bay for a year in Toronto, finishing a two-year floral design course. She'd graduated with honours and returned home to work in her family's flower shop. Seven months had passed, and she couldn't even guess what her best friend was thinking.

He looked the same, mostly. Now twenty-one, he was still taller than her. In his snug Henley shirt, he was broader and more muscled than his year-ago self, his dark hair more stylish. His green eyes and his smile were unchanged. She wanted to reach out and stroke his jawline, to feel the bristle of his beard, the softness of his mouth.

She gasped and knotted her fingers together, trying to steady her breathing.

These new and disturbing urges were all the fault of her college friends. They'd ogled pictures of Denis and teased her mercilessly about "gettin' me some of that". Of course, Shelby knew he was handsome. She had eyes, after all. She'd just never thought of Denis that way.

Until now.

Now it seemed like she couldn't stop thinking of him that way.

He was her best friend.

He was not supposed to make her breath catch or her heart thump or her palms itch to touch him.

But he did. Oh, he did.

The duo who was playing tonight came back onstage. Julia and Izzy were locally famous for entertaining the crowd with renditions of 1940s and 50s crooner songs.

Beside her, Denis stood and touched her arm.

She tipped her head back.

"Want to dance?" He spoke with the French accent of Northern Ontario.

"Sure." On the dance floor, they moved into their familiar position, close but not too close, friends, not lovers. They'd danced together dozens of times, teaching each other how to find the beat and keep the rhythm. She'd stopped his geeky shuffle, and he'd stopped her flailing arms. They were such good friends. She sighed.

Think of something else!

She grimaced at the memory of this morning's fierce argument with her mother. That worked.

Denis squeezed her hand, drawing her attention. "What's up?"

She rolled her eyes. "Mom."

"What's your mom done now?"

"She won't let me make my cousin LeeAnn's wedding bouquet because she doesn't trust me not to screw it up. She keeps telling me we have to be careful with such 'delicate and expensive blooms' and 'birds of paradise have to be soaked and opened just so' and 'make sure to wrap them as instructed' and blah blah blah. You'd think she forgotten that I aced my course."

Shelby's parents owned Affodell's Florists; Mom was the florist and Dad handled everything else. Shelby grew up surrounded and fascinated by the ritual of turning bunches of cut flowers into creations of beauty. She didn't need Mom being all judge-y.

Denis gave her a quick hug. "She needs time to believe in your work. You know what you're doing, Shel."

Shelby grinned up at him. What would she do without her best friend, always on her side, always supportive and cheering her on?

The song ended, and the crowd clapped.

A guy bumped into Shelby, shoving her against Denis. Her breasts pressed against the hard wall of his chest. His arms tightened around her. Tingles zipped and zapped along every single one of her nerves. Denis's quiet moan tickled her ear.

Good grief, she must have stomped on his foot. She stepped back and bumped into the person who'd bumped her in the first place. "Sorry," she said to both Denis and the other guy. "Cramp in my foot. Sorry."

The clumsy jerk turned back to his girl.

"This sucks. Let's go back to the table." Without waiting for an answer, Shelby wriggled through the crowd and plopped down into the chair furthest from the seething dance floor.

Denis sat beside her, his thigh brushing hers. More zipping and zapping.

Shelby jumped up. "Gotta go to the ladies' room." Then she ran as if zombies were on her tail. Slipping into a stall, she leaned against the back of the closed door. What was wrong with her? Why was she going all tingly over Denis?

He was her best friend, not her—whatever.

Shelby sighed heavily, used the facility, and left the cubicle to wash her hands. She tugged at her Raggedy Ann red hair; a cool idea gone horribly wrong. And now her blond roots were showing. Argh! What the heck had she been trying to prove?

Kerri, a girl from her old crowd, came into the ladies' room. Her hair was naturally red, and naturally curly, and naturally disgusting when combined with cute clothes on a cuter body. Kerri checked for feet under the stall doors. "Yeah, good, we're alone. I wanted to talk with you."

"Yeah? What's up?" Shelby propped herself against the counter, expecting some juicy gossip.

Kerri poked around in her purse, dug out a red lip gloss, leaned into the mirror, and applied the gloss with careful strokes. She side-eyed Shelby's reflection. "So, Shel, you like being back in Clarence Bay, yeah?"

"Yeah, sure."

"Are you, well, you know, good with Denis?" Kerri cut another glance at Shelby.

Shelby gripped the counter. "Of course I'm good with Denis. What kind of stupid question is that?"

"Not stupid at all. He's a handsome guy with a respectable job as assistant manager at the hardware store. He's decent and knows how to treat a girl. Who wouldn't go out with him?"

Shelby blinked, then shook her head to clear her ears. "What?"

"Well, he went out with other girls while you were at flower school, so we all figured you were, like, doing the same. You know, like, shopping around." Kerri replaced the wand in its tube. "Yeah?"

"Uh… sure, I went out." Not for lack of trying and not very successfully, but no way was Shelby admitting it.

"So, we were all—" Kerri rolled her eyes and pressed her hand to her heart, "I—was wondering, now you're back, if you and Denis are, like, together, you know?"

Shelby swallowed hard to ease the sudden tightness in her throat. She pretended to check her mascara. "No, we're not dating." She glanced at Kerri's reflection. The sudden grin on the girl's face pinched Shelby's heart. Why should Kerri's interest in Denis piss her off so much?

"So it's, like, um, okay if I ask him to a Christmas party? To, you know, get back with him?"

"Back with him?"

Kerri blushed and fiddled with her purse straps. "Yeah. Of all the guys I dated, he's the best. I want him back."

Anger like Shelby had never known swelled from the pit of her stomach and stopped her breath. Hands trembling, she turned on the water and let it run cold over her wrists. The chill did nothing to ease the anger. She stared at herself.

Why?

Why was she so angry at Kerri for wanting Denis? They were both her friends. They'd make a cute couple. Why shouldn't they get back together if they wanted to?

Because.

Because Shelby *did* want Denis in that way. She wanted him as her *own* boyfriend.

No, not boyfriend.

Lover.

She wanted to love Denis. Make love with him.

She pressed her cold, wet hands to her cheeks.

What had she done?

"So, Shel, that's okay with you, yeah?" Kerri's voice wobbled.

Shelby straightened and faced Kerri. "No, it's not okay."

Kerri jammed her hands on her hips. "He's going out with someone else?" Her voice rose to a squeak of surprise.

"Not yet."

"He *told* you something? C'mon, you gotta tell me. I gotta know my competition."

You're looking at her. "He didn't tell me anything."

Kerri narrowed her eyes. "But you know anyway. It's not fair you're so tight with him. I say you're keeping him for yourself."

"*Pfft.* I don't think so." Shelby yanked on the door handle and escaped.

Denis Corbeau scanned the tavern. No sign of Shelby yet. *Sacré.* How long could he stand being near her and still pretend to be nothing more than her good friend?

Good friend. Ha!

What kind of good friend wanted to kiss his friend silly? Kiss her until her knees weakened, and she melted against him. Kiss her until she begged him not to stop.

Denis curled a lip in disgust at himself.

A creep of a good friend. That's what kind.

What was wrong with him? Why did the press of Shelby's breasts against his chest make him moan like an idiot, make his dick push against the zipper of his jeans? Why did he dream of her soft, naked skin against his own?

Chien. Dog, he was such a dog. He shook himself, trying to get rid of the thoughts. But the thoughts clung like water on a dog's thick coat.

Across the room, Shelby's neon red hair glared under the lights. His mouth tightened. What had been wrong with her beautiful blond hair? She said it was all about showing her independence. He sighed. As a show of independence, the dye job was an epic fail. It was a good thing nobody, especially her mother, could see her other declaration of independence. Hair could be cut off or re-dyed. A tattoo was forever.

His shifted on the hard wooden chair.

A morning glory vine now twined its way up Shelby's back, from her left butt cheek to her right shoulder blade. He hadn't seen it in real life though, only in photos as the tattoo grew. The last photo had damn near killed him; Shelby peeping over her shoulder right into the camera with a sly, naughty expression that haunted him. Fierce heat flowed into his cheeks. *Chien.*

He reached for his glass of beer, hoping for at least a few cool sips to calm him down.

Kerri tapped his shoulder. He jumped so hard; he lost his grip on the glass. The last bit of beer swirled across the table.

"I'm so sorry." Kerri sprang into action, whipping paper napkins out of her purse and mopping up the mess. She stuffed the soggy blob into the glass. "I didn't mean to startle you." She laid a hand on his shoulder.

Denis shrugged her hand off. "I was just thinking about something."

"Or someone? Me?"

No, not her. He met begging brown eyes in a sweet face surrounded by soft red curls. How to stop this? Music penetrated his frantic brain. "Dance?"

Kerri's smile lit the dark room.

Sacré. He'd given her false hope. Denis called himself every name in the book, in English and French. Hold on. Why false hope? Kerri was cute, a nice girl. He could do worse than go out with her again. It wasn't as if he was dating anyone else. And he wanted a girl he could get to know, grow to love, maybe even marry someday.

A flash of fake red hair announced Shelby's arrival. "What are you doing?"

Denis couldn't recall Shelby ever giving anyone the murderous scowl she was throwing at Kerri. He expected Kerri to drop his arm and jump away from him. Instead, she slid her hand down his arm and took his hand in hers. Brave girl.

"We're going to dance." Kerri tugged him away.

Shelby reached for his free hand as he moved past her.

The group of six other friends around them stilled. Their gazes flicked from one girl to the other.

"Chick fight," a guy said.

Shelby blasted a fiery glare at the dumbass, growled at Denis, and dropped his hand. "All yours," she grumbled.

Kerri returned Shelby's earlier scowl with interest. "We don't need your permission. He's not that kind of friend, you said. Remember?"

Grinning like an idiot, Denis followed Kerri. Why he was grinning, he didn't have a clue.

Once they reached the dance floor, Kerri placed his hands on either side of her waist, wrapped her arms around his neck, snuggled up close, and shuffle-swayed to the music. Her curves were pleasant against him, soft and sweet. But something was missing.

He lifted his gaze. At the now empty table, Shelby sat with her arms crossed, staring at him and Kerri, a dark frown on her face. Suddenly, she grabbed a couple fistfuls of her hair and tugged hard, as if she wanted to yank disturbing thoughts right out of her head.

A crazy yearning to rush over and fix things for his dearest friend surged up. He'd always fixed stuff for her; the chain on her bicycle, a flat tire on her car. But this time, there was nothing to fix.

Shelby pressed her fingers to her mouth and lifted her gaze. Their eyes met and held. Were those tears reflecting in the light? Denis dropped his arms from Kerri's waist. He didn't want to *fix* anything for Shelby. He wanted to love her and have her return his love.

Ça suffit! Enough! Shaking off Kerri's frantic clutching, he moved towards Shelby, ready to end this stupid "just friends" thing. As their feet hit the edge of the dance floor, the lights went out and the tavern went dark.

Before anyone could complete "What the...?" the lights were back on. On stage, Julia didn't miss a beat, continuing to sing Elvis's "Can't Help Falling in Love".

Shelby saw him coming, saw the concern in his eyes. She jerked around, away from that look of his. If she wasn't careful, he'd be hovering, thinking he could fix it for her. The trouble was… a confusing mess of conflicting emotions.

"Shel, what's wrong?" Of course, Denis was there, at her side, in her face. He stood close, generating a current of emotion between them.

"Nothing. Just a headache. And cramps. You know." Lame lie, but it worked.

Denis backed away, hands up in surrender. "Okay. No problem. Did you want to go home?"

"No way. I'll be fine. I just need some painkillers."

Kerri, who'd followed Denis, intruded. "Why didn't you ask for some Midol in the washroom?"

Really? She had to say Midol? "Thanks, I'm okay."

"Good." Kerri grabbed Denis's hand to drag him back to the dance floor. "No wonder she's so bitchy tonight."

The lights flickered again, went out, and this time, they stayed out. Julia and Izzy carried on with their performance, unfazed by the lack of power. No electricity was needed for an acoustic piano and a good voice.

Five minutes later, the fun of dancing in the dark wore off. People got antsy, stopped dancing, and started muttering. Phones came out… nothing happened… towers must be down. Flashlight apps came on like lightning bugs on a summer night.

Moving cautiously, with Kerri glued to his side, Denis went to the door to peer out. The entire town was in darkness. There was no light at all—no Christmas lights, no streetlights—nothing glowed to fill the black hole of their hometown.

"The whole town is out," Denis reported to the group inside.

A shrill whistle ripped through the moaning and groaning of the crowd. The tavern's manager stood on the stage. "All right, folks. It's close enough to call closing time. Get yourselves together and get on home. I'll see you all tomorrow when the power is back on and it's business as usual. And before you go, let's give a big hand to tonight's awesome performers, Julia and Izzy."

Those who were fans clapped enthusiastically, while others searched for their coats. With a bit more whining and some excited whispering, the dancers and drinkers filtered out into the parking lot.

Denis twisted to search the room, deftly releasing himself from Kerri's unwanted grip. Where was Shelby? He had to drive her home. There. He waved her over.

Kerri made a show of looking around. "I came with a bunch of my friends, but it looks like they left without me. Nice friends, eh?" She gave him one of those help-me looks. "Can I bum a ride with you?"

A quiet snort of disbelief came from beside him. Shelby had joined them, coats in hand. Denis glanced her way. She handed him his parka, then got busy wrapping her scarf around her neck.

"Uh, sure, I guess so."

Kerri grinned, huge and a bit smug.

"I'll drop you off on the way to Shelby's place."

Her grin slid away to be replaced by a scowl at Shelby. Shelby returned a tiny smile full of gloating. Denis ignored the tension between the two young women and focused on finding his keys. It was awkwardly cool to be the object of desire in a chick fight.

Tossing her red curls over her shoulder, Kerri grabbed her own coat and purse. "Let's go," she said, tucking her arm through the crook of his elbow.

Their crowd was rowdy in the darkness, hooting and hollering as they piled into vehicles and drove away, leaving the parking lot in utter darkness. Clouds drifted away, allowing the almost full moon to lay eerie shadows over the humps of snow. Off in the distance, a pair of car horns blared through the night, strange beasts fighting over an intersection normally controlled by a traffic light. Sheesh, change the least little thing and people lost all sense of how to act normal.

"C'mon, Denis. I'm cold." Kerri pulled on his arm.

They crossed the parking lot to his truck. Denis unlocked the door and Kerri made a big show of clambering in to sit in the middle of the bench seat, leaving Shelby to shuffle through the fresh snow to the other side. Denis shrugged and got behind the wheel. Kerri sat so close; she was almost in his lap. The whole trip, he was pre-occupied with keeping his arms tight to his sides to avoid elbowing her in the chest. If she thought he was getting hot and bothered, she was wrong. More like good and annoyed. On the other side of his unexpected passenger, Shelby spread her arms and smirked at him, clearly entertained by his predicament.

At last, the way-too-long-for-a-short trip was over.

Kerri made Shelby open the passenger door and climb out. Once Kerri had Denis to herself, she leaned over, squeezed him high on his thigh, and laid a fast kiss on him. "See you tomorrow, handsome," she said in a carrying voice.

"Uh…yeah." Of course, they'd see each other tomorrow. Kerri worked as a cashier at the hardware store. Why did she make it sound like a date?

Kerri climbed out of the truck, gave Shelby a smug hair flip, and went into her darkened house. Shelby slid in with a tight frown on her face, eyes pinched with accusation.

Maybe it wasn't such a cool thing to be at the centre of a chick fight.

The power was still out when they pulled into Shelby's driveway. No light flowed into the truck from the fixture over the garage door. The Christmas lights strung along the eavestrough didn't glow in welcome. As usual, Denis turned off the engine and they sat quietly for a few minutes. One of them would start talking soon.

Shelby twisted her fingers in her lap. She glanced at Denis, who stared out the front window. "This is weird," she said.

"I wonder when the power will come back on?" he said.

"Long before we wake up." Why the heck were they going on about a stupid power outage? "So, are you going out with her?"

"*Quoi?*" At last, he turned his head to look at her.

She rolled her eyes at him. Guys were so obtuse sometimes. "I think she still has a thing for you."

"Nah. We already went out and broke up."

"So she said. Why didn't you tell me?" Which hurt more, him keeping a secret or the nature of the secret? Or both?

He dug his hands into his pockets. "You were in Toronto. After me, she went out with some guy from Orrville. After him, it was a guy from Bala."

He hadn't answered one of her questions.

"Then why is she making eyes at you again?" She pushed for an answer.

He shrugged, long and loud. "Dunno. Maybe she hanged her mind and wants to get back with me?"

"Do you want to get gotten back with?" She tsked at herself. "You know what I mean."

A smile flashed across his face. "I know what you mean."

Her heart sank at another unanswered question. Where had their openness gone? She shivered as cold crept into their cozy place. She should never have gone to Toronto.

Without looking, he twisted the ignition key to turn on the heater. Warm air blew from the vents. It didn't help much as her cold was inside.

He hung a wrist over the steering wheel and tapped his fingers on the dashboard. He drew a deep breath. "Shelby?"

She waited for him to carry on, or at least turn to look at her. After a crazy long silence, her patience wore out. "What?" she snapped.

His feet shifted. "Do you think we have a good…uh…relationship?"

She sagged back against the seat in huge relief. "Of course we do."

"You don't think it could get better?" He faced her, his eyes solemn. His gaze dropped to her lips.

Shelby sat very still. Her mouth tingled. She licked her lips. He did the same.

"Denis?"

His gaze met hers, intense and hot. He slid across the bench seat and caressed her cool cheek. Warmth spread from his gentle fingers.

Her eyes slid shut.

And popped open.

Denis's face was centimeters from her own. He tipped his head and leaned towards her.

Her heart seized with fear. She grabbed for the door handle and scrambled out of the truck, almost falling into the snowdrift beside the driveway.

"No! Our relationship couldn't be better. It's perfect as it is." She slammed the door against his surprise and ran into the dark house.

Once inside, she leaned against the closed door. She banged the back of her head on the hard wood. "Why am I so stupid?" she whispered harshly.

"Is that you, Shelby?" Mom called from upstairs.

"Yeah, it's me."

"Everything okay?"

"It's all fine." How did Mom know she was upset? Mom ears, that's how. In the thin light from her phone, she lit the candle Mom had set out for her, then took off her coat and boots. Cupping the candle's flame like an old-timey heroine, she climbed the stairs, oblivious to the cold air. She was plenty warm from something she didn't want to name.

Three Days Before the Wedding

"Shelby, wake up." Mom shook her by the shoulder.

"*Mumph.*" Shelby burrowed under the covers. After tossing around most of the night, she needed more sleep.

"It's past nine o'clock. You're scheduled to go into the shop."

"Nine?" Shelby rolled over and flipped off the covers. At the chilly blast of air, she hauled the blankets back.

"Shelby, get your butt out of bed. We've got customers waiting for their Christmas table arrangements." Mom tugged on the blankets, but Shelby refused to release them.

"How'd it get so late?" She craned her neck to see the blank face of her digital alarm clock.

"The power is still out. And it will be for a few more hours according to the *Beacon*'s emergency info line. Your dad and I slept in, and he's got to hit the road to Toronto for our flower shipment. LeeAnn's birds of paradise are in that load, and her mother will have a fit if we don't have them. She's got her heart set on those blooms."

"Mom, please let me make up LeeAnn's bouquet. I know how to prep birds and I really want to do this for my cousin."

"Why are you so obsessed with doing her bouquet?"

Because I owe her, big time.

Another tug of war over the blankets ensued. Shelby won again.

"We've been over this before. I'll be doing the bouquet. If anything goes wrong, not that I expect it to, but if it does—*I'll* deal with my sister-in-law, not you. She's turned into such a ridiculous control freak."

"Please, Mom?" Shelby put all the little girl begging she could into the words. She even added big pleading eyes.

"Please, will I make you some toast and coffee while you shower? Sure." Her mom swotted Shelby's butt through the thick layers of blankets. "Now, get going. Good thing our stove and hot water tank are fuelled by gas," she said on her way out.

Shelby flipped back the covers and indulged in some heel kicking and hand pounding. "Argh! Why won't she let me do it?! Why?!" She raised both her arms and legs, flapped them around, and dropped them spreadeagle to the blankets. Ugh! So not fair! After dragging her butt off the bed, she took a steamy shower and shivered her way into chilly clothes. They may have had hot water, but they didn't have any heat in the house!

Downstairs, Mom was talking to Dad while he put his boots on. "Grampa Bill and Grammy Wendy are doing fine for now. They've got plenty of firewood and Grammy's using the barbeque to cook. Grampa's full of stories from when he was a kid."

"At least when he goes on about his adventures during the Ice Storm of 2013, we'll know what it's really like to live without power," Shelby said.

Mom and Dad both chuckled. "Nice one, kiddo. I'll have to tell that to my brother when I see him," Dad said. He slung his coat over his shoulders and stuffed his arms in the sleeves.

"Drive careful, John." Mom tucked his scarf around his neck and got a big kiss in return.

"I will." He ruffled Shelby's hair.

"Hey! I just styled that!" she protested.

He grinned. "Stay warm, my girls." A blast of icy wind swirled into the kitchen as he opened the door and headed out. Shortly afterwards, the old panel van roared into life.

"So, Shelby, there are five arrangements for delivery tomorrow... do your usual marvellous job. I'm going out to make sure Grampa's not telling stories about how they're doing. I expect the power will be on before I'm back. On the way home I'll call on your brother, then I'll come and help you. Okay?"

"Sure. Say hi to Tyler for me." She waved Mom off, finished her breakfast, and hustled out to her small red Honda. The snow squeaked under her tires in the bitter cold. On the way downtown, with the dazzling blue sky and the bright sun reflecting off the snow, it was hard to tell the power was out. Donning her sunglasses, Shelby drove carefully, watchful of black ice.

As she entered the street-level floor of the building housing the family flower shop, she flipped the light switch a couple of times. Of course, no power. What a pain. Sighing, she hung her coat in the staff room. She shoved up the sleeves of her heavy sweater as she went to the front of the shop. Checking the orders, she saw the usual roses, carnations, and greens. Oh, and look, an entire shipment of poinsettia. *Bo-ring.*

LeeAnn's bouquet was to be made of exotic bird of paradise blooms.

Shelby frowned.

It ground her gears that Mom still *helped* her, making sure she did everything just right.

Shelby had owed LeeAnn big time for a long time and Shelby wanted to pay her cousin back in any way she could. She didn't have any money or other assets. Even her car really belonged to her parents. All she had was skill and talent to create the most beautiful bridal bouquet ever seen in Clarence Bay. It wasn't much in exchange, but something was better than nothing.

Of course, Mom didn't know about The Incident. Only the three of them—LeeAnn, Shelby, and her brother Tyler—knew.

Shelby continued to wrack her brains while stripping leaves, clipping stems and slipping them into flower frogs or foam, crafting table arrangements to cheer any Scrooge. Even after a couple of hours, with interruptions to serve customers, she still hadn't come up with a way to clear her heavy moral debt.

Fan-crappy-tastic.

She needed to talk to somebody. She reached for her phone… Damn. Plenty of battery, no signal. Her hand hesitated over the handset of the landline. She needed her best friend's advice and sympathy.

Before she dialed, she had to search for Denis's number on her cell phone. Pushing real buttons was plain weird. Only there was no answer on his cell. Well, duh. Try the hardware store. Another search. Sigh. How did people manage in the days before the internet?

"Good morning. Chisholm Hardware. How can I help you?" Kerri said in a super-perky voice.

Shelby rolled her eyes. "Hi, Kerri. May I please speak with Denis?"

"Sorry, Shel. He's with a customer right now. May I take a message?"

Was Kerri lying to keep Shelby away from Denis? "No, that's fine. I'll catch him later. Have you got heat in the store?"

A frustrated sigh gusted down the line. "No! And it's such a pain to have to write out receipts, like, with a pen. And carbon paper. Well, that's kinda cool. People are buying so much stuff. It's taking forever, and my hand is sore, and my car didn't start."

"Poor you."

"Denis picked me up."

Shelby could almost hear the smug hair flip. Her hand clenched with the urge to reach through the wire and snatch the naturally curly red hair right off Kerri's head.

Bitchy much?

Shelby swallowed down the jealousy churning in her throat. "Nice of him."

"Oh, yeah, I called, and he came right over. He's such a great guy. But you know that cuz you're such good friends with him."

"Yes, he's a great guy. Well, would you have him call me, please?"

After saying goodbye and hanging up the landline—more weirdness—Shelby picked up an arrangement to store in the cooler. Instead of the usual gust of fresh chilly air, it smelled stale and stinky. The rest of the stock was wilting. She checked the thermostat. Off, of course. Hmm, why was it so warm? It didn't make sense. She shrugged. Dad would check it out when he got back. She walked to the front window as if it would make him show up.

It was still blindingly bright outside. When would the power come on? And what about those flowers? They had to stay cool, or they'd start wilting and cost the shop a lot of money. Mom had insurance, but still… Wonder if Denis could fix the flower cooler?

As if she'd conjured him, Denis passed on the sidewalk outside. The shop bell jangled when he pushed the door open, letting in a blast of arctic air.

Joy surged up from her heart and rushed along every nerve ending, spreading heat along the way. She barely stopped herself from running into his arms. She was always happy to see her best friend, but this sensation was off the charts. Way off. Why was she reacting like this?

She pushed down the sleeves of her sweater and pulled her hair out of its ponytail.

Why was she fussing over her appearance? It was just Denis.

Denis tossed his mittens onto the counter and tugged off his toque. He ruffled his thick dark hair a couple of times, but it stayed flat. Winter hat hair, such a treat.

Her hands reached for him. Stupid hands. Get down.

"You alone?" he asked.

She gulped, nervous. Like he'd asked her a tough question. "Um, yeah."

"Something's bugging you, Shelby." It was a statement, not a question. He knew her so well. He cupped her shoulders, a thing he'd done lots of times.

This time was different.

She met his gaze, and her world shrank to the space between them and the look in his green eyes. The friendliness in them faded along with his smile. His pupils flared, intense and focused on her.

"Shelby?"

She opened her mouth. No words formed in her mind. Emotion, pure unnamed emotion, swirled through her.

Denis touched her cheek. The chill of his fingers startled her from her stupor. She stepped back and shook off the tangle of feelings.

Desire?

For her best friend?

Nah. Must be the weird unpowered world they were living in. Nothing was normal. She sure wasn't. Her recent worry came back to her. "The cooler is broken." She pointed a vague finger over her shoulder.

Denis's face slackened. His shoulders slumped; his head dropped as if in defeat.

"Can you fix it?" She ignored her friend's body language.

Denis's mouth tightened and he squared his shoulders. When he met her gaze again, he looked so sad. "It's not broken. The power's out."

Face, palm. She knew that. She couldn't think of anything else to say. "Will you help me move the stock to the back hall? It's chillier there and they'll stay fresher. Leave the table pieces. I'll call people to come pick them up if they can."

Denis drew a breath as if to say something.

Without thinking, Shelby shook her head slightly.

Denis let out his breath and nodded. "Okay. For now. Let's move those flowers."

❄

A while later, nicely warm from all the shuffling back and forth, Shelby picked up the shop's ringing landline.

"Shelby, it's Mom. LeeAnn's wedding is postponed."

"What do you mean? What's happened? Is LeeAnn okay? Jesper?"

Beside her, Denis stiffened to attention.

"Everyone's fine. Why would you ask?" Mom said sharply.

"Remember LeeAnn's dad?" Shelby's heart rate slowed from its 100-meter sprint. Three years ago, LeeAnn's first wedding was postponed because her father had passed away from a sudden massive heart attack.

"Oh." Mom tsked at herself. "Sorry I frightened you, sweetie. Everyone's fine. The truck broke down and Dad can't get home with our flowers, including LeeAnn's birds of paradise. He's staying with his brother until they can fix the truck. I've called her mom and Norah said with no bouquet and no power, she's cancelling the wedding."

Shelby scanned the shop. "We have lots of flowers here, Mom."

"Not the ones that Norah wants."

"What about what LeeAnn wants?" Shelby tried to remember what LeeAnn's choice had been during the customer interview. "Didn't she first ask about something Christmasy?"

"Hmm." Mom thought for a minute. "I don't quite remember. But birds of paradise are what they ordered and paid for."

"Can you wait a bit, Mom? Let me see what I can do with what we have left in stock?"

"Don't trouble yourself, sweetie. Let's wait and see if Dad can make it home. We still have a few days. It'll be tight, but I can do the bouquet."

"What if he can't make it? Or he does, and it's too late to soak and open the birds, then what? Let me try, Mom. I want to do this for LeeAnn. I don't care what Aunt Norah says." Shelby paused at the image of the fierce freak controlling her aunt. "Maybe you should call LeeAnn instead?"

Mom chuckled. "Nice workaround, kiddo."

"So, you'll let me do it? Make LeeAnn's bouquet?"

Mom paused. "Does it mean so much to you?"

"Yes, Mom, it does."

"I sense there's a story here…"

Shelby didn't reply. Someday soon she'd be spilling the belated beans about the incident on the train tracks.

Mom's resigned sigh hissed along the line. "Okay, I'll think about it. Tell me about the arrangements you've done for today's orders."

Shelby sagged. One small step for daughter-kind. She told Mom about the cooler going wonky, and her and Denis moving the stock to the back hall.

"Good idea. That's the perfect spot. Clever you. Is Denis still there?"

Shelby stared at the handsome guy leaning against the counter, patiently waiting. He winked at her. He'd never done that before. Was he flirting? She looked over her shoulder at the empty store. He grinned as if he knew what she was thinking. Her heart dashed off again.

"Shelby? Are you there?" Mom's question startled her back to their conversation.

"Uh. Yeah. We're both still here."

"Excellent. He'll see you home safe. The weather people are all in a dither about something called a polar vortex collapsing. Like we need more aggravation. Cold is cold."

"Sounds lovely." Shelby grimaced. "How about I choose the flowers for LeeAnn's bouquet, set them aside in a labelled bucket, and then we can talk design specifics?"

Mom chuckled and sighed her surrender. "Okay, okay. It's a plan. Have fun and say hello to Denis for me."

Shelby hung up and punched the air. "Yes!" She added a hip-swivelling victory dance. "Yes, yes, yes."

Denis grinned. "You're making LeeAnn's bouquet, *non?*"

Overflowing with joy, she threw herself at Denis.

He caught her easily and pulled her close. Even through her thick sweater and lined jeans, she felt the strength and planes of his chest and the long muscles of his thighs. Heat blasted through her. Desire followed in its wake. She snatched her arms from around his neck and planted them on his shoulders, intending to push away from the shock of his touch.

He loosened his grip but didn't let go.

She stared up into his green eyes. His pupils were large, and his breath, short. His gaze dropped to her mouth. Her lips parted. He lowered his head, then hesitated and looked into her eyes. His lips formed words she couldn't make out.

And finally… he kissed her. A light, quick peck that left the impression of soft warmth. She held her breath, waiting, wanting.

Denis held his breath as he looked down into Shelby's blue eyes to gauge her response to his boldness. Her eyes widened with some emotion, her mouth opened in a surprised little, "Oh."

So he kissed her again, deeper this time. He savoured the taste of her—a taste he'd been longing to sample for months now. Sweet. Like the roses she handled every day. Her lips were as soft and pliable as those petals. He deepened the kiss, bringing her closer, shaping her against him.

Her arms tightened around him, and he exulted in her desire. She pushed her hips against his, and his dick thrust to meet her belly.

The strong pulse shattered the sphere they inhabited.

She pushed and he let her go. "Denis. No." She crossed her arms, her sharp elbows taking the place of her soft breasts.

"Why?" Disappointment howled like a lone wolf.

"We're friends. Good friends. The best." She stepped back, wiping his kiss from her mouth with a brush of her fingers. "I can't lose my best friend."

"I'm not going anywhere."

"Not yet."

"Not ever. Is it not possible for friends who love each other to become lovers?" He stretched out a hand, silently pleading with her to take it. To become his.

She looked down at his palm, then up into his eyes, and slowly shook her head. "I can't risk it. You're too important."

"We can risk it together. You know I would never hurt you." He raised his hand higher.

"How can you say that? How do you know what the future will bring?"

"There are no guarantees. There is but trust." He stroked her cheek. "Do you trust me, *ma chère?*"

"Completely." Her gaze dropped; and she turned away from his touch. "It's me I don't trust."

Two Days Before the Wedding

"How about if I place the roses like so," Shelby added some swirls to her sketch, "and the carnations like this." She added some starry shapes. "There are baby's breath and asparagus ferns left. Add a gold wired ribbon, *et voilà*—a new bouquet for LeeAnn." With a flourish, she drew a rudimentary bow. "What do you think?" She slid the sketch across the coffee table.

Shelby and her mom sat in front of the gas fireplace in the living room, the faux logs and the brick surround now the only steady source of heat in the house. With leggings under jeans and heavy sweaters over flannel shirts and thick tees, they were comfortable enough. Mom had unearthed fingerless gloves. Last night, they'd dragged a double mattress from the spare room to share by the fireplace. They'd also rigged a blanket across the arched foyer opening to contain the warmth. After porridge cooked on the gas stove, they made tea.

Mom studied the sketch. "The *Beacon*'s social media says it's still not known how long the power will be out. Toronto is down now, too. No sooner does the power company fix one line than another line gets snapped by a fallen tree or broken branch. The power crews are stretched to the limit. The province asked for volunteer linemen from everywhere in Canada."

Shelby frowned at Mom's non-reply to her floral design. That was okay—ish. While she had Mom's attention, there was other information she wanted. "Did you know Dad very long before you got married?"

Mom went quiet, staring into the distance, calculating. "Three and a half years before we got engaged, then another ten months before the wedding, and just so you know, another fifteen months before you were born." Mom stiffened and her gaze went laser sharp. "Any particular reason you're asking for these numbers now? Do you and Denis have something to tell us?"

A blush scorched its way up Shelby's chest and into her face. "No," she choked out, adding a wild headshake for emphasis. "Denis and I are friends. Only good friends, BFFs."

Mom relaxed against the back of her chair though her gaze still questioned. "Too bad. If you ever need to tell, or ask, me anything, I'm here for you."

"Thanks, Mom." So embarrassing!

"I've always liked Denis."

Shelby's feet shuffled under the table as if they wanted to run. Shelby couldn't agree with them more. "Is there a point to this discussion?"

"Not really. I just wanted to tell you that your dad and I are here for you."

Silence fell. The gas fire hissed. Bright sun streamed through the windows, adding solar heat to the room.

Mom knocked on the table. "It's a good thing Chloe's finished LeeAnn's wedding dress. Norah showed me a picture. The dress is long, very poufy and princessy."

Shelby sagged in relief; no more talking about Denis. Though, oddly enough, that's all she wanted to discuss. "Long? I thought LeeAnn wanted a short one."

"So did everyone else." She shrugged. "But Norah talked her into going long and poufy."

"Her mom has gone total control freak."

Mom nodded in resigned agreement.

"So, about LeeAnn's bouquet?" Shelby tapped the sketchpad and held her breath against Mom's expert commentary.

Mom stroked a finger along a spiral meant to be a rose. She sighed.

Shelby's hope tanked.

"I think it's lovely. Exquisite. The school taught you a different way to think about flowers. LeeAnn will be a lucky bride to carry this bouquet. When it's ready, I want you to take some photos for the website. The local brides will come flocking. Maybe we'll even get a few city girls coming in. I hope there's still a charge left in the camera battery."

Shelby's chest swelled and her eyes teared up at Mom's unexpected high praise.

Mom smiled, wry and questioning. "Did you think I'd hate your design?"

Shelby nodded.

"I've watched you playing with flowers since you were old enough to pick one. I've spent years teaching you everything I know. Now it seems the egg can teach the chicken a few things." Mom patted Shelby's hand. "Finish your tea and get down to the shop."

A half-hour later, under heavy grey clouds pushed along by blustering winds, Shelby rushed into Affodell's, eager to make her design a reality. By instinct, she flipped the light switch, then groaned.

"My flowers, it's cold in here. Almost colder than outside." She shivered hard and rubbed her arms. "Cold enough to make ice cream. Cold enough to make ice cubes. Cold enough to freeze the balls off a brass monkey. Cold enough to—" She gasped. "No!"

Tension screwed her shoulders tight as she hurried past the useless coolers to the back hall where she froze in her footsteps.

"Oh. My. God." The sketch fluttered from nerveless fingers to the cold tile floor. She lifted a shaking hand to her trembling mouth.

Every single bloom, every arrangement not picked up, had frozen solid, brown and ugly, with bare hints of the colours that had glowed yesterday.

Her shoulders slumped as her vision of the perfect bouquet for her beloved cousin vanished. With the vision went her hopes to show her mom she was a freaking goddess with flowers.

Goddess? Exaggerate much?

Dragging her feet, she went behind the front counter to call her mom. All that money lost and their clients disappointed. Mom took it philosophically.

"Nobody could have planned for a power failure like this. I'll deal with the insurance company. Clean up as best you can and come home."

"But what about LeeAnn?"

"I'll call Norah. I love my sister-in-law, but sometimes… You tried, sweetie. Put your design in the folder. Another bride will enjoy your bouquet when we have more stock."

After Mom gave her a few more instructions, Shelby hung up and slouched on the stool.

The shop bell jangled over his head as Denis opened the front door to the flower shop. Ryan, the owner of the hardware store, had shut down for the duration of the power outage, so Denis was free to do what he wanted. He wanted to be with Shelby and here he was, looking at her gloomy face.

He slipped off his parka and put it right back on. "*Sacré*, it's cold in here." He stepped around the counter and took her in his arms. She drooped against him. He held her closer and kissed the top of her head. "What's wrong, *ma chère?*"

She groaned and pointed around his torso towards the back hall. "All the flowers are totally destroyed, frozen."

"*Sacré.*"

She straightened. "I'll say. I finally had Mom convinced to let me do LeeAnn's bouquet and now I've lost my chance." Teary eyes stared up at him, begging him to make it right.

He tucked a stray lock of her hideous rag-doll hair behind her ear. "Have you told your *maman?*"

She waved a listless hand at the landline. "Just now. She took it in stride."

"*Bon.* What happens to the frozen flowers?"

"I take pictures of them for the insurance company. They're frozen into the buckets, so clip off the tops, throw them all in the compost bin, then stack the buckets in the sink to thaw whenever the damn power comes back on."

"What does your cousin LeeAnn say?"

"She doesn't know yet, but she's going to be so disappointed. My mom's calling her mom to tell her the oh-so-fabulous news."

Denis struggled with the grin her sarcasm provoked. No need to make Shel feel worse. "Will the wedding be postponed again? Jesper will not be happy."

"I dunno. Depends on how cranked Aunt Norah gets." She heaved a huge sigh.

His gaze glued to the thrust of her breasts. The rest of him noticed as well. *Chien.* Dog. He forced his gaze to her face and choked.

Her gaze was glued below his belt. She licked her lips.

His dick responded with a wild bounce. "You're killing me, Shel."

"Huh?" She blinked and lifted her head. "Oh, my flowers." She pressed her hands to cheeks so red they must hurt. "I'm sorry. I—" She jumped to her feet. "We've got a mess to deal with," she said over her shoulder as she rushed away from him.

He'd wanted to ease her disappointment, maybe get more than one kiss. Instead, he'd chased her away. Shoulders slumping, he dragged his feet after her.

They tidied up as best they could. At least they got warm from the exercise. They were about to head home the late-afternoon dark when the shop landline rang.

"Hi, Jesper. I guess you heard the news about the flowers?" Shelby said.

He huffed a rough laugh. "Yeah, no kidding. Norah is going ballistic and ranting about postponing the wedding. She's forced LeeAnn to agree, which I'm not happy about, but you know what Norah's been like lately."

"An out-of-control control freak?"

Another rough laugh. "You got that right. Listen... LeeAnn and Mrs. Hadley are stuck with us out here at the farm, and I want to ask you a huge favour. Can you make another bouquet? Use whatever you have. It doesn't have to be flowers. Just make it pretty and bridal."

"Uh…"

"LeeAnn's crying…"

"I'll do it."

"Wonderful. Same time and place as on the invitation, the Festival Hall, Saturday, four o'clock."

"If you're stuck, how will you get there?" She tossed a bug-eyed look at Denis.

"That's my problem. One more thing, don't tell LeeAnn. It's a surprise. Okay? And whatever you do, don't listen to anything her mother says. Okay?"

"Uh, yeah, sure."

"Gotta call Julia and Tyler for the music and food before the tower goes out again. See you." He hung up.

"Bye," Shelby said to the dial tone. "How do I do that?" she said.

"Do what, *ma chère?*"

"Make a bridal bouquet without flowers." She held a hand to her mouth. "The Christmas Spirit was listening and gave me this chance."

"*Quoi?*"

"Jesper wants a bridal bouquet for LeeAnn. And you know why I have to do everything I can for her, right? Why I owe her?" Shelby had told him about the train track incident the day after it had happened. LeeAnn had been a hero.

He nodded. "*Je me souviens.* So, where do we find more flowers in winter with one day's notice?"

Shelby's gaze jumped around the shop then settled on him. "There's nothing left here, so I guess we're going hunting tomorrow."

One Day Before the Wedding

"Go for a cross-country ski, she said," Denis grumbled to himself. His breath created a frosty mist in the cold air. "It'll be good exercise, she said." He jabbed a ski pole hard through the ice to gain purchase in the snow beneath. "The snow will be so pretty, she said." After temperatures rose above zero yesterday afternoon, the falling snow had turned into freezing rain, coating the world with brittle, sparkling ice. "It'll be fun, she said." Behind him, he towed a kid's old-fashioned wooden sled with a laundry basket tied to the seat.

"We're going to find something better than imported flowers for my cousin's wedding, she said," he continued. "We're going to harvest nature's bounty, she said." The wedding was tomorrow, and it was almost noon. Every surface was treacherous with ice, every move was made at slow speed.

"Personally, I say it's a good thing it's so fricking cold out here, so nobody can see me making like a donkey."

Shelby skied ahead of him along the fitness trail that ran through town. She'd stop, cross her arms, and assess something. She either snipped it off and loaded it into the basket or turned up her nose and kept skiing.

He stopped to remove a glove to dig out a tissue. The sled bumped over his skis, clipped the back of his boots, and bounced off the path. He flumped down on his hands and knees, giving his neck a nasty jerk.

"C'mon, Denis," Shelby called.

He grunted as he got to his feet, finished with the tissue, and slid his glove back on. Groaning, he hauled ass along her new-laid tracks.

She waited impatiently with another armload of stuff for the basket.

"Please say you've got enough."

Hands on her hips, tipping her head from side to side, she inspected her odd collection. It looked more like stuff for the compost pile to him. But what did he know? He was just the donkey here.

"Almost. There's a dogwood up ahead. I can add some colour with the red branches. Then we can stop at the lookout for lunch. Okay, Eeyore?"

He grinned crookedly, gestured for her to take the lead, and trudged along behind her. Just for fun, he brayed. Her laughter floated back to him and warmed his heart.

After harvesting an armload of red branches, they skied on to the rest area overlooking the wind-scoured ice-covered bay. After they unlatched their skis, Denis handed her the insulated picnic bag and Thermos jug from behind the laundry basket. Then he spread a blanket over the snow-covered seat. She poured hot cider while he unwrapped chicken pieces and plastic boxes of peas with salad dressing. They had no bread since the grocery stores were all closed. No power meant no cash registers meant no food from the store.

It was the best meal ever.

"Don't you think Jesper is a bit crazy, thinking he can pull off a surprise wedding in the middle of a massive power failure?"

"I think it's romantic."

He huffed. "Sure, it's romantic… if it doesn't all fall apart."

"True. But I'll do whatever I can to make it happen. I hope he managed to call Julia and Tyler before he loses signal again."

"Julia and Tyler?"

"Music and food."

"Of course."

"I have no clue what Julia plans to sing or play or whatever. Tyler converted to solar last year, so at least he can cook. He's sure to come up with something incredible to eat for LeeAnn's reception."

"If your brother is cooking, the food will be fantastic." Denis leaned back and stretched his arm along the back of the bench, as he always did.

Normally, she would lean against him. Instead, she turned in her seat to gaze at him. Her knees pressed against his thigh.

He didn't say a word, but he let his love for her show in his eyes.

She huffed out a breath, like a little dragon. Her pupils widened and her neon-red hair blazed in contrast to the grey day. Huge flakes began to drift down.

He smiled provocatively, let his eyes drift shut and waited, daring her to kiss him. He heard the rustle of her nylon coat as she moved. The sudden chill on his thigh gave him a millisecond's warning before the snowball hit him in the chest, spraying ice-cold shards down the front of his jacket.

Several feet away, she laughed as she balled more snow.

He sprang to his feet and floundered after her, capturing her as she drew her arm back, ready to launch another missile at him. Scooping her close, he trapped her folded arms between them and gazed down at her. The merriment faded from her eyes and questions filled them.

She opened her mouth to speak, but he stopped her words with a kiss. He slid his tongue into her sweet warmth for a moment and withdrew. Looking down into the dazed blue depths of her eyes, he kissed her chilly nose. She blinked and seemed to come to herself. Her stiff spine softened, she leaned into him and raised her face, asking for more kisses. And he willingly gave them, there in the early twilight of a snow-filled sky. Flakes swirled and floated around them in the profound silence. Denis wrapped her more tightly in his arms and put his whole heart into his kiss, telling her how much he'd grown to love her, how much he would always love her. Still, he dared not say the words. The last thing he needed was for her to pull back, brushing off the kiss, forcing them back to being just friends. Reluctantly, he released her and set her back on her feet.

"Denis…"

He pressed a finger across her mouth. "*Ne dis rien.* Let's get all this stuff back to the shop so you can make the perfect bouquet for LeeAnn."

Shelby gazed to the side into the sparkling snow. She nodded.

They picked up their gear, latched on their skis, and slid back onto the path home.

Back at the shop, Shelby pretended nothing had happened. She gathered her forest treasure and spread it over the work counter. Bunches of red berries, branches of red osier dogwood and corkscrew willow, sprigs of blue-green spruce and delicate white pine. There followed a plundering of the ribbon supplies and silk poinsettias. She built, took apart, and rebuilt until she was satisfied, and her fingers were so cold she couldn't feel them. The final touch was a tiny parcel tucked where only LeeAnn would see it.

"All done. What do you think?"

"If I were ever a bride, I'd be proud to carry it," Denis said. For that, he got a big grin from Shelby. She burrowed her icy hands under his sweater to warm them against his skin.

He yelped and snatched her hands away. "You're frozen. Let's get you back home, yes? I'll put the bouquet in the truck, and you lock up."

"Yes, please."

Once at the house, they entered through the back door. Compared to the deep freeze outside, the unheated indoors was almost cozy. A note on the table drew her attention. *Shelby, I've gone to the Hadley grandparents. There's stew ready to reheat in the oven. Back soon, Mom.*

Shelby showed Denis the note and they took off their coats. Denis set the table while Shelby went to turn on the gas fireplace in the living room. She halted at the blanket-hung doorway, eying the mattress, complete with fluffy pillows and puffy duvets.

A sudden awareness that Denis was in the house, steps away from an inviting bed, sizzled through her. What would it be like to make love to him? Heat flowed from her belly outwards. Shaking it off, she stepped gingerly around the bed as if it might blow up if she wasn't careful. She bent to turn on the fireplace.

"Shel, are you coming?"

Shelby squeaked and jumped guiltily at Denis' voice from the doorway.

He stood stiff as an icicle, staring at the bed. His gaze rose to her face, and he flushed bright red and swallowed.

She gestured toward the fireplace. "The fireplace makes it warm in here and the—uh, blanket keeps the room warm. The blanket across the door." She babbled on, unable to shut herself up. "When Mom comes home, we'll sleep together tonight. Me and Mom, that is. You'll—uh—you'll go home to your own bed. Where you'll—uh—sleep. By yourself. Not with me. Though if you were to stay—" She clamped her mouth shut.

From either side of the fluffy expanse of white flannel sheets and feather duvets, they stared at each other. Her blood thumped in Shelby's ears. She'd practically invited her oldest and dearest friend to sleep with her. As in, spend the night between the sheets.

Together.

Naked.

And other stuff.

Denis cleared his throat. The quiet sound boomed around the room.

She jumped. "Yes?"

"Your mother will be home soon. *Non?*" Disappointment tinged his voice.

Her shoulders slumped. "Yes."

"I thought so."

"Stew?"

"*Oui.*"

In silence, they retreated to the kitchen and settled at the table. Later, by the fire, they drank tea and coffee, ate cookies, and played childhood card games. Shelby cheated and Denis let her, as always. Through the laughter and silly games, thoughts of The Bed throbbed between them. Darkness settled in and worry rose as an almost-welcome distraction. The landline rang loud in a lull in the conversation, startling them and sending cards skittering across the coffee table. A hand pressed to her thumping heart; Shelby answered the phone.

"Shelby, it's Mom. I'm out at Grammy and Grampa Hadley's and I'm stuck in the snow."

"Do you want me to call someone?"

"Don't bother. We're fine here. How about you? Did you find the stew?"

"Yes. It was delicious."

"You'll have to spend the night on your own. Sorry, sweetie."

Shelby glanced at Denis sorting cards. Her throat tightened. "Uh… no problem."

"Your voice sounds funny. Is everything okay with you?"

Oh, my flowers. Mom could always tell. "I—uh—can you keep a secret from Aunt Norah?" She offered up the lesser of two secrets.

"Ye-es."

"LeeAnn's fiancé called me."

"He did? What did he want?"

"He asked me to make a bouquet for LeeAnn."

"I thought they cancelled the wedding."

"Jesper wants to surprise LeeAnn and have the wedding anyway, same time, same place. The invitation still stands."

"That's a risky decision. So much could go wrong. How will they all get there? How will all the guests get there?"

"Don't you think it's romantic?"

"*Humph*. What about the food and music?"

"Julia and Tyler are helping him."

"Good luck to them. And Jesper. He's a good man and deserves someone like LeeAnn after all he's had to put up with from his future mother-in-law. I hope you brought the bouquet home with you."

She touched a gentle finger to the tiny gift. "Yep, it's here with me now. Safe and sound."

"Just like you."

She looked over at Denis. He straightened. "Just like me."

"You're all set then. G'night, sweetie. I'll see you in the morning, or at the wedding, or sometime soon." Mom sighed. "Take care of yourself."

"I will. Take care of yourself and Grammy and Grampa. See you in the morning."

Shelby hung up and Denis rose from his cross-legged position on the floor. She walked to him, slid her hands into his ready clasp, and stared up into his eyes. His smile lit the green depths, heating her blood and bones.

He nodded, encouraging and answering at the same time.

"Will you stay with me tonight?"

"*Oui, je resterai*," he said with all the solemnity of a vow.

A spasm of trepidation seized her and cemented her feet to the floor.

"Nothing will happen you don't want to happen. *Je promets*. I promise."

"I want everything to happen. But—"

"You're afraid of wrecking our friendship if we do this," he said, a statement, not a question.

"What if it doesn't work out? We won't be able to go back. Will we?" she asked.

"*Non*, I don't think so. But if we do nothing, we won't stay the same either."

Stay the same and risk their friendship for fear. Or go forward and risk their friendship for love. They'd tried avoidance, awkwardly dancing around each other since she'd come home. It hadn't worked very well. Was it time to try love? "If this doesn't work, will it be the end of everything between us?"

"*Non, ma chère*. Nothing will end. Nothing will fail because we know each other so well. Our future is safe. *Je t'aime*. I love you, Shelby."

His strong, softly spoken conviction bolstered her own.

"I love you, Denis." She pulled his arms around her, then slid hers around his neck, and tilted her face for his kiss. She didn't have to wait long.

Denis pulled her closer until her breasts pressed against his chest.

She wiggled her hips against his and he groaned like he was in pain. She grinned to herself. She might be a virgin, but she did know stuff.

He slid his hand under her sweater and found another sweater, and a flannel shirt, and a ribbed t-shirt, and a camisole. He growled. "How many layers do you have on?"

She laughed at his frustration. "As many as it takes to stay warm. No power. Remember? I've got leggings under my jeans, too." A sudden painful shyness seized her. She couldn't meet his eyes. Gentle hands cupped her shoulders.

"I've never done this before either," he said.

Surprised beyond belief, she blurted, "The girls in this town are stupid."

He laughed and shook his head. "*Non, ma chère*, they are not. I was waiting for you. I want you to be my one and only lover."

She giggled. "That must have been har—difficult."

He replied with a very French shrug. "You are worth it."

She beamed up at him and raised her hands over her head. "Will you help me get this stuff off?"

They took turns removing layer after layer until he had only his briefs and she her camisole and panties.

Shelby's shyness returned. She'd only ever seen infants and small boys naked. He slid his thumbs under his waistband, blew her a kiss, and stepped out of his briefs. Amazing how much a small bit of fabric could cover.

"Please, *chérie*, will you show me your tattoo?"

She crossed her arms briefly then dropped them. Turning her back, she slid off her panties to show the base of her tattoo curling over her left butt cheek. She swivelled her hips, grasped the hem of the camisole, and slowly lifted it. Denis gave a low moan. Good to know all her silly practice in front of a mirror was paying off. Then it hit her. She'd been practicing for Denis all along.

She peeped over her shoulder. Denis stood stock still except for one body part that bounced a greeting. It was kinda embarrassing. His smile encouraged her on. She gathered up the fabric of her slip-on bra and camisole, pulled both garments over her head, and dropped them on the floor. She peeped over her shoulder, watching his eyes follow the vines as they curved from her left hip, twining across her mid-back, and stopping in full bloom on her right shoulder. Smaller blooms and leaves filled the spaces in between. One tendril went around her waist. Uh, she'd never practiced what came next.

"What—" he croaked, then cleared his throat. "What kind of flowers are they?"

"Morning glories. My hair is supposed to be the top flower."

"Ah."

"Epic hair fail, eh?"

"If you let your hair grow out, it will soon be blond again, and be the sun for your flowers." He rolled his eyes as if he couldn't believe how stupid his idea was.

"That's so sweet." She grinned at him and turned around.

They gaped at each other in full frontal nudity, plus socks.

Grinning deliriously, they stepped close to each other. Or they tried. His erection poked her soft tummy and kept her at a dick's distance. They looked down, looked up, and choked on their guffaws.

A sudden shiver seized her, and she dove under the blankets. He followed after grabbing the condom from his wallet. Amid sighs and soft laughter, they learned the ways their bodies moved. Then instinct took over and they joined, cautiously, joyously, for the first time.

THE WEDDING DAY IS HERE

Shelby awoke to heat like she'd never known. Her back nudged against another back. So naked and so hot.

Denis.

Her best friend and now her lover.

She rolled over to cuddle his back. She tried, and failed, to keep her hand still. They'd never touched one another in a sexy way. His skin was smooth, his muscles relaxed. Her feet stroked against the hairs on his legs. He stirred and tipped his face up to her, a sleepy smile in his eyes. Then, he shifted onto his back and took her in his arms. She laid her cheek against his shoulder, her hand on his heart.

A really awkward pause descended.

"Uh, I have to pee," she muttered.

He gusted a sigh of relief. "Me, too."

She kissed his shoulder and ran to the washroom. She shivered through the necessities and dove back under the covers. Denis was out and back in moments. She warmed him by climbing on top of him. He cupped her butt, and she swivelled her hips against him. He groaned happily and lifted his head for a kiss.

The slam of the kitchen door and the sound of voices filtered through the blanket-hung doorway.

Shelby whipped the covers over their heads split seconds before Mom, Grammy, and Grampa entered the living room. Three loud gasps confirmed their arrival.

"Shelby Jane Hadley, what are you doing?"

Shelby stuck her head out, careful to keep Denis covered. "Sleeping?"

Mom's mouth quirked and laughter creased her eyes. "I hope that's Denis Corbeau under there. Otherwise, you have some explaining to do."

Denis lowered the blanket, showing a very red face. "*Oui*, Mrs. Hadley, *c'est moi*."

Mom jammed her fists on her hips. "Well, it's about time you two got yourselves sorted." She turned and shooed her in-laws towards the kitchen. "I'll make breakfast while both of you get dressed." Mom stopped and eyed the bouquet. She moved closer to examine it, touching the tiny gift box.

Shelby's nerves tensed under the scrutiny of her work. Mom faced her with a teary smile. "I now know what my daughter's future holds. Shelby will be safe with Denis, and my flower shop will be safe with Shelby. Well done, Shelby. Well done. Love the little gift."

Shelby teared up. "Thanks, Mom."

Hand at her throat, Mom headed for the kitchen.

Shelby grinned down at Denis. "Let's go. We've got a wedding to attend."

WINTER'S HARMONY

Stormy Wedding 2

Four Days Before the Wedding

Marshall Rickerts stood centre stage on the polished boards of the Festival Hall, gazing over the rows of seating and up into the shadowy rafters. To his left, folding glass doors in stone-faced walls framed an impressive view of a frozen Clarence Bay rimmed with snow-covered trees. The glare dazzled his eyes. "Great hall, Reg. I heard that all the seating folds into the floor," Marshall said to his tour guide. The reverberation of Marshall's words demonstrated the excellent acoustics.

"That's right. The stage we're standing on can be lowered to main-floor level as well. An incredible bit of engineering," bragged general manager Reginald Barker, a tall man, bald, with a luxuriant walrus moustache. "During the music festival, it's in this configuration—all seats up, stage up. We're about to break it down for a wedding on Saturday, so stick around for a couple of days if you want to see it."

"I might." The length of Marshall's stay depended on the success of his other mission in this small town with a big musical reputation; his mission to find Pearl. "You have a practice room, but not formal change rooms?"

"Right on both counts. Our local theatre group uses meeting rooms for changing, and the practice room as the green room.

Most musicians come dressed to perform. The gift shop in the lobby sells CDs and branded merchandise on commission."

Marshall nodded. "Standard procedure for a smaller venue." He turned in a full circle, scanning the seats wrapped around the entire hall at the mezzanine and balcony levels. "What sort of town is Clarence Bay like to live in? Musical?" He fought to keep his voice to a bland curiosity.

"All of our music is in the festival. To be honest, we didn't even have an accredited music teacher until two years ago."

"Oh?" Marshall prodded though he knew the answer.

"The stellar Carlotta Pentland moved here when her career ended. Back problems, you know, sitting at the piano for hours at a time."

Marshall's back twinged in sympathy. Disappointing intel. The whole music world had witnessed her forced retirement. "Must be exciting for the town."

"At first, we all went a little celebrity mad, you know. Now we're used to it. Sometimes, a summer tourist gets weird, you know. We had an unpleasant incident this year with a crazy fan. Miss Pentland was very upset. She went in disguise for a few days. What can one do?" He shrugged. "We can't hide the fact she's here. The internet, you know. We just don't tell folks where she lives. She's one of *us* now."

"So that's why I can't find my old friend."

Reg's eyes narrowed in suspicion. "You're a friend of hers?"

"We shared teaching gigs at a few summer education programs." Passionate memories from those four years delighted his mind's eye.

"The town is very proud she chose to live here. And we're happy to protect her as well. Like I said, we don't give out her address—no matter *who* you say you are." The man crossed his arms over his well-muscled chest.

That put Marshall in his place. He smiled to himself. Good to know she was cared for. "Do you know where I can meet her in a public place?"

"No. We can't watch over her *that* closely. Much too intrusive." Reg walked away. "You wanted to view the practice space?"

"Yes, please." Marshall followed him to a door in the corner of the hall. "This is the perfect spot to end the summer season next year, when we'll be back in Canada and close to home base in Toronto." Frustrated though he was at the lack of information about Carlotta, Marshall understood and admired the town's good intentions. But, damn it, he wanted to meet her. Even if she might not be keen to meet him despite their history.

After dealing with the paperwork for the Quâtre Jazz Quartet's appearance, they passed through the offices again. Marshall spotted a whiteboard listing the booking schedule for the different rooms. He searched in vain for Carlotta's name, hoping she'd be drawn to play in a space with such fabulous acoustics.

Pearl.

Heat bloomed in his chest and spread through his body. Could this Pearl be Carlotta using the nickname he'd given her? And was it significant?

Heart thumping, he promised himself to return tomorrow morning and find out.

"And that's the hour, Asher." Carlotta rose with ease from the chair beside her Steinway grand piano. "Excellent work."

"Thank you, Carlotta." Asher was the only one of her students to call her by her given name; all the others called her Miss Pentland. He was also her only adult student. He gathered his pages of scribbled music, a composition of his own. He tapped a musical score, sitting on the round table in the middle of the room. "Wagner's 'Bridal Chorus' and Mendelsohn's 'Wedding March'? Are you playing them for LeeAnn this Saturday?"

"I am."

"Aren't they a little stately for LeeAnn? Don't you see her wanting something more casual?"

"I completely agree, but her mother insisted. 'If it's good enough for Queen Victoria's daughter, it's good enough for *my* daughter.' A direct quote. Do you know the Hadleys?"

"Not as well as my wife Emma does. The Finns and Hadleys are part of the Settlers of Clarence Bay. That's how Mrs. Hadley says it—with capitals. Anyway, LeeAnn and her mother were in Emma's shop choosing china, and they almost came to blows."

"No!" Carlotta raised a hand to her open mouth. "Who won?"

"Jesper broke the tie and sided with LeeAnn."

She smoothed some stray white strands of hair behind her ear. "Good man."

"It's a wise bridegroom who sides with his bride rather than his mother-in-law." Asher's dark eyes crinkled with laughter. "This town sure does love its gossip." Asher had moved to town around the same time as Carlotta, and they'd had several discussions about newcomers as fresh fodder for the grapevine.

"Don't we all? LeeAnn is a lovely girl. She treats me like I'm a favourite aunt." Carlotta pretended to scratch her nose to hide an unexpected welling of tears. "It's a novel experience for me. I will always be grateful to her."

"She's Brendan's grade-two teacher. My son has a serious crush on Miss Hadley."

"Aw. That's so sweet. LeeAnn's mother is something else though. Very controlling, I understand."

"I'm glad she's not *my* mother-in-law." Asher zipped up his music case.

Carlotta walked with him to the entry, then stood in the archway of the music room of her centre-hall house.

"Are you all set for the coldest winter in decades? Do you need some firewood chopped?" Asher shoved his feet into his boots and shrugged into his coat. "Those weather forecasters get a kick out of exaggeration, don't they?"

She joined in with his chuckle. "I'm all set. Thank you for your offer, though. I appeared in Budapest in January one year and the power went down for a day and a half. Everything got so cold, so fast. And they still expected a performance from me. I wore long johns under my gown and borrowed a mink coat, but I performed. I was never so happy to leave a venue, especially since my next stop was Monaco."

Asher laughed. "Jacques Corbeau warned us long before the weather people figured it out. Something to do with a heavy crop of acorns for the deer out by his place."

"There's nothing like an old-timer's forecast. I'm ready for it. I have a cord of firewood in the shed, cans of soup in the cupboard, and candles on the mantle. That should hold me for at least a few days."

Asher smiled and headed for the door.

"Goodnight, Asher. Have a lovely warm Christmas holiday on St. Lucia with your family and I'll see you next year."

With a sigh, Carlotta shut the door behind the last student of the day and the year.

Asher blinked the headlights of his car as he pulled away and headed home to his wife and two boys. He wasn't her average student, being an adult, an ophthalmologist no less. He played and composed for the pure pleasure of it, and occasionally entertained his family and friends. Carlotta commended him for knowing his limit and living within it.

What would her life be like if she'd chosen Asher's route? Chosen family over career?

A lot less lonely, she expected.

She shuffled through her music, putting together the selections for LeeAnn's wedding in four days. Since moving to Clarence Bay, she limited her performances to special favours for special people, the occasional stint at community fundraisers, and her student recitals.

She envied Asher his unadulterated pleasure in music. For her, music had been a life-consuming job. A job of giddy highs when hundreds of pairs of eyes were focused on her and weary, lonely lows when the applause ended, and her adoring public went home. Her chronic back pain had almost been a blessing in disguise. Now she got to move around, exercise, walk, shop, whenever she wanted. No longer was she compelled to sit on a hard piano bench, practising for hours a day. She was pain free for the first time in decades. Physiotherapy and yoga were marvellous things.

But… how she missed the joy of sharing her gift, the wonderful people she met, the beautiful cities she visited, and the historic venues where she followed in the footsteps of virtuosi like Mozart, Liszt, and Chopin.

She released a heavy, resigned breath.

Tomorrow, she would go to the Festival Hall to run through the selection a few times to get a feel for the instrument and the room. Her own piano was a superior instrument, but you couldn't beat the sound of a building with perfect acoustics.

She went to the kitchen and came back with a full watering can to take care of her trio of poinsettias.

A sudden noise outside shattered her calm. She dropped the watering can, splashing her jeans and soaking her carpet.

Was the stalker back?

Her heart jumped into her throat, and her nerves tightened. Squelching across the wet spot on the carpet, she snapped off the room's lights. Groping around the furniture in the sudden darkness, she grabbed a flashlight from the table in the front hall and moved cautiously through the kitchen towards the window in the door.

The police had assured her the person had been escorted to the border and their passport flagged. Had they been able to slip back into Canada along the vast, unprotected 49th parallel? Would anyone be so obsessed?

From behind the lace curtain, Carlotta strained her eyes to penetrate the gloom of a winter's evening. The motion-sensitive yard lights flashed on, glaring off the snow and deepening the shadows. She blinked rapidly.

A hump-backed creature waddled across a patch of gleaming snow on the way to the compost bin in the distant corner of the garden.

A raccoon.

Carlotta sagged in relief against the cold glass. She must remember to properly fasten the lid of her compost bin. She flipped on her interior lights and went back to her task, humming snippets of Asher's joyous piece. After mopping up the spill and placing LeeAnn's, or rather Mrs. Hadley's, selection in her briefcase, Carlotta settled in front of the television.

"The collapsing of the polar vortex continues to wreak havoc across the nation. Regions of Northern Ontario are under a winter storm watch with high winds. Southern Ontario can expect freezing rain. Get your flashlights and candles ready, folks, and make sure the woodpile is stocked up."

Three Days Before the Wedding

The next morning, Carlotta awoke bursting with energy. Bright winter sun streamed through her window and her busy day called her out of her snuggly bed. She threw back the covers and rose. A frigid blast of air drove her back into the warmth.

"Good grief." She glanced at her alarm clock and saw a black rectangle where bright green numbers should be.

Great. A power failure.

Bracing herself, she leapt out of bed, dashed to the bathroom for a quick visit, grabbed her wristwatch off the dresser, and scrambled back under the covers.

"Nine o'clock. No wonder I feel so rested…" Her stomach growled, and she chuckled, "…and hungry."

After dressing in layers and wrapping a fleece throw over her shoulders, she went to the kitchen and feasted, sort of, on milk and sandwiches. How she missed her hot morning tea. From the list of emergency contact numbers pinned to her kitchen notice board, she called the town's information centre.

"You have reached the Clarence Bay emergency information line. Power outages have occurred across wide areas of the province. A state of emergency has been declared. All power workers have been called to work. Power is estimated to be out for eighteen to twenty-four hours in some areas. As usual, The Festival Hall, the Community Centre, the high school, and both churches are operating as shelter centres for those without heat. Call this line again for updates on the hour. In the meantime, stay safe and warm. Further instructions are available on our website at ClarenceBay.com or refer to the emergency information pamphlet distributed to all households."

Curious, Carlotta searched for the pamphlet and found it in the junk drawer in the kitchen sideboard. She found information on the safe usage of wood fires, propane heaters, and generators, how to spot hypothermia and frostbite, and how to cook over open flames and on wood stoves, and lots more she thought she'd never need—until now. So, that's how you banked a fire. Huh. No time like the present.

Just as she settled in front of her crackling fire in her comfy chair under a duvet, Carlotta's glance caught on her briefcase. Good grief, she'd forgotten all about her practice session. Reluctantly, she banked her fire as instructed, and drove carefully through the snow to the Hall.

The three-storey foyer of the Festival Hall echoed with the cacophony of men rolling stacks of folding chairs and tables. More men unfolded and arranged them. Urns for coffee and tea occupied stations in several locations around the perimeter of the room. People bustled about setting out trays of sandwiches and cookies. Sunlight, pouring in through the floor-to-rafter windows, lit the activity. A gigantic Christmas tree filled a corner by the northeast window. Wreaths and garlands decorated the stair railings to the upper floors.

Reg, the general manager, bustled up to her. "The main auditorium is full of people, so we moved the piano into the practice room. I know it's not the same acoustics, but at least you'll be able to, um… hear yourself play." He grinned a tad smugly at his small wordplay. "And you'll be plenty warm. We've got generators and solar panels for backup, so we'll be comfortable for the duration." He sighed and gazed out the window where heavy clouds gathered on the horizon. "Provided the duration isn't too long."

"At least it's warmer here than at home." Carlotta dodged busy people and running children to enter the practice room. She slipped out of her coat, then hefted up the grand piano's lid to the fully open position. Seated on the padded bench, she ran a glissando from the lowest bass key to the highest tinkling note. As expected, perfectly in tune.

She ran through her standard warm-up routine and played through the music. For some unknown reason, she'd never performed Wagner's "Bridal Chorus", so her fingers didn't have it committed to muscle memory. She had no pain in her back. How wonderful. Once she was satisfied with her performance, she went on to play one of Asher's compositions, a joyful sonatina with a serene and flowing second movement, bouncing to a sparkling allegretto finale. She finished with a flourish. As the final notes faded away, she lowered her hands to her lap.

Clapping from the far end of the room startled her. She turned to stare at a chapter of her fading past come to hearty life in the present. Her fingers tangled and twisted. She'd never expected to see Marshall again. Guilt still chewed at her conscience almost twenty years later. She drew a fortifying breath.

"Brava, my Pearl. Brava," Marshall cheered.

Guess bygones were bygones. Carlotta's tense shoulders relaxed as she rose from the bench and walked towards him. He was a little slimmer than back in the day and a wee bit stooped, as if life lay heavy on him. Cautiously, she placed her fingers in his outstretched hands. His hands cooled hers, hot from her work. Up close, sadness muted his sparkle.

"You see, we *are* friends," Marshall said to Reg with a sidelong smirk.

"Yes, this liquorice stick is an old friend," she said, calling him by the nickname given to all jazz clarinetists. She smiled at the marketing director. "Thank you for looking out for me so well, Reg. Marshall should have let me know he was coming, so I could have let you know."

"Can't be too careful." Reg scowled at Marshall. "I'll leave you now as I've many other duties to attend to." He gave a brisk nod and marched off.

"What did you do to annoy him so much?" Carlotta asked. His gentle tug drew her closer. Without thought, she turned her cheek for his kiss. His scent filled her head with heated memories.

"Nothing but make arrangements to view the Hall as a venue for the quartet." He shrugged. "And claim you would recognize me on sight. I hoped to surprise you."

"Well, you succeeded with your surprise."

An awkward silence stretched to fill the room.

She looked pointedly at their joined hands.

He slowly withdrew his clasp, as if he didn't want to let go. "How are you?"

"Unnerved." She still couldn't take in that Marshall was standing before her.

He nodded. "Good word. Says it all for me, too."

Carlotta walked over to the enormous windows and stared out at the wind-scoured landscape, the aching blue of the sky. All of the other men in her past had been so easy to brush off. But not this man. This man had always gotten her to say more than she meant to reveal.

His footsteps echoed on the wooden floor as he followed her. A careful hand rested on her shoulder, as if he was asking permission to touch her. Considering what they had once been to each other, the gesture was harmless enough. She allowed herself to lean against him for a moment, to take the friendship he offered. Then she straightened and stepped away. No sense in getting comfortable.

"Why are you here in Clarence Bay?" she said. For revenge? After all this time? For love? After what she'd done to him? Not likely.

He waved his arm to encompass the building. "To view the venue and to see you."

She ignored the second reason. "You've never performed here before? I find that hard to believe for a Canadian quartet to not have played the well-known Clarence Bay Festival."

"I'm not sure why we haven't. Guess the timing was always wrong... until now. Now, it's perfect." He lifted his hand, palm up, in a clear invitation.

Ignoring his gesture, she asked, "What do you think of the Hall?"

He stepped back with a wry face, clasped his hands behind him, and turned to the view. "The staff is supportive and well-organized, the acoustics deserve their accolades, and the view is incredible. I think the group will like it here." He hummed a few bars of music; the same few bars he always hummed while he tried to figure out what to say next.

Surprised she remembered his quirk, she smiled to herself.

"You went out on a high. Your last performance was memorable, moving, masterful." Sincerity sang in his voice.

Her smile faltered, recalling the simultaneous highest and lowest points of her life. Three standing ovations, two encores. Followed by an aching aloneness that sharpened her physical pain. Unable to bear his pity, she stared back at the icy view. "You were there?"

"I had to be."

"I wish I'd known."

"I couldn't stay for the after party. My wife needed me. She passed away two months later."

"I'm so sorry for your loss." The trite phrase was all she could think to offer.

"It was, as they say, a blessed release." He grimaced.

She glanced sideways up at him. His face was drawn and sad. "Your children?"

He brightened. "Our eldest, Aidan, is doing his PhD at MIT. Our second, Serena, is first violin with a Toronto orchestra. Our third child, Laura, is an artist. Well, she's not a child; she just gave me my first grandson. Time flies. The youngest, Eric, is an architect. He has a daughter on the way."

Fierce emotion, hard to name, surged through her. Envy? Regret? Longing for what might have been? She was all alone in the world—no siblings, no parents or grandparents, no aunts or uncles, cousins, nieces, or nephews. And now she was too old to have her own babies, even if she'd had someone to make babies with. Her career had been everything in her life. And now she was too decrepit for that life.

A heavy cloud moved across the sun. The bleak cold of winter chilled her to her soul. She shivered, hard and deep, and wrapped her blue cardigan tighter around her body.

"Why did you leave the stage?"

"The pain was too much. Too many hours sitting in one position. Tendons tightened; muscles weakened. I walked—shuffled—like an old woman from frozen hip syndrome. The painkillers ruined my performance. So many stupid mistakes. I had no choice. Perform poorly or perform not at all. I collapsed after that final performance." Collapse was such a small word for what happened.

He wrapped an arm around her shoulders and pulled her close. His heat soothed and rattled her. Her eyes filled with tears. She leaned into his strength, sought his compassion. His other arm came up to cradle her against him while grief for her lost self wrenched her heart. How could this man get her to let go of the tears she'd held in check ever since she walked off the stage for the last time?

Long minutes later, she groped in her pocket for a tissue. "Sorry." She gave a watery laugh. "I'm being pathetic. It's not as if I lost someone I loved. Not like you."

He frowned at the snowdrifts on the deck outside. "No, but your music was more dear to you than any person."

"My first season without performing was hell on earth. I had no place to be, no practice, no purpose. And there was so much pain. I didn't know who Carlotta Pentland was anymore." She blew her nose. "I went to physiotherapy, took up yoga, Pilates, and swimming." She huffed a sarcastic breath. "Who learns to swim after fifty? What a life I had as a youngster." She fished out another tissue and mopped up more tears. "I stopped playing, didn't listen, didn't go to concerts. I couldn't bear it. I cut music out of my life." She met his gaze, defiant. "And I was glad. Carlotta Pentland, world-renowned piano soloist, was *glad* for the silence."

He tipped his head back towards the piano. "The music didn't stay gone."

"No. I couldn't leave the music after all. I needed to occupy myself, and it's all I'm trained for. Now, I'm just a lowly piano teacher." She chuckled, dry and wry. "I'm a dreaded 'Do I *have* to go?' teacher."

"You're neither lowly nor dreaded. You are *the* Carlotta Pentland when all is played and done."

She laughed lightly at his pun and gave him a quick hug. "You're right. I have a new purpose. Now, I perform for my students and for special people."

"Like brides?"

"Only one bride, who is a dear friend." LeeAnn had opened her heart and her community to a stranger.

"Any new composers? The final piece was beautiful."

"An adult student of mine, Asher Stockdale, wrote it for his wife. He was kind enough to give me a copy of his score."

"I've never heard the name before."

"That's because he plays and composes for the pure joy of it. He's an ophthalmologist in real life. I envy his passion. And the fact that he doesn't have to play for his supper. I teach his son as well." She laughed, thinking of the frustrated young boy she'd seen at their last lesson. "I don't think the boy has inherited his father's talent. Perhaps his brother has it."

"Any promising talent elsewhere in this little town for you to nurture?"

"Possibilities are plentiful, but no prodigies. Then again, I'm not quite sure how I'd like it if one did appear."

"You don't want to find and develop a protégé?"

"It would be lovely to pass on my skill, but I hesitate to introduce someone into such a taxing, neurotic, and lonely world." She shrugged. "But here I am, preaching to the converted." She stroked his arm. "Tell me about your group."

"Now that I've accepted the engagement here, we're booked solid for the next year."

"Good for you. I'll look forward to seeing you play."

"Will you?"

She was about to return a flippant reply but the yearning in his eyes, as if her answer was important to him, stopped her.

"Umm…." She rushed to fill the silence. "And I'd like to invite you to be my guest at the wedding on Saturday. If you're still here."

Marshall drew back, surprised by the invitation.

Why? Had he expected something more intimate? How ridiculous it was for him to think they could pick up their relationship like it was yesterday instead of last century.

"I'd be delighted. Is this the wedding you were practicing for? Don't brides go for something more modern these days? My son's fiancée turned up her nose at Wagner. So two centuries ago!"

She laughed. "I wouldn't know what the modern bride wants. The bride's mother insisted." She turned mischievous eyes up to him. "They pay, we play, darling."

He laughed aloud at the old joke from the second summer of their relationship. "Do you remember Clive?"

"Who could forget him? Any idea what happened to that cynical young man?"

"He went to Manitoulin Island to live with his true love. They're raising goats for cheese and mohair. And he's no longer cynical."

They chuckled together, slipping into their old way of talking. Their relationship had begun with a chance meeting back in the day when they'd both been teaching at a summer program for advanced students at a Boston college. Their professional lives had pulled them apart and drawn them together for several delightful summers. Their final summer, just as her career rocketed to new peaks, he'd asked her to marry him. She'd chosen music over marriage.

"May I take you to lunch?" He held out his hands and waited.

She stared down at his hands. Where might this overgrown path lead? Did she want to find out? With a tender smile, she put her hands in his, then almost yanked them back. Finally, her hands settled in his, palm to palm. "Yes, please."

It sounded like a promise of so much more than lunch.

Carlotta, followed by Marshall in his own car, cautiously drove avoiding the chunks of dirty ice left behind by other vehicles. Once inside Cherrystone's, the family diner that locals called The Pits, they removed their coats and sat down at an empty table. Carlotta set her music case and purse on the chair beside her.

Glory the manager approached. "Good afternoon, Carlotta. How are you getting on without power?"

"Oh, I'd forgotten about the power outage," Carlotta blurted, a blush burning its way up to her hairline. "I've been practicing at the Hall and Reg had their generators going." She squared her shoulders, well-practiced at looking calm and collected even when she was a twitching mess of nerves.

Glory nodded as if she actually believed her. "That explains it. Our solar panels are good, but we still need to conserve energy, so I can offer you natural lighting and grilled food. All kinds of creatively grilled foods."

A young woman with long chestnut hair and deep dimples joined Glory. She vibrated with excitement and a nervous smile.

Carlotta prepared herself for a fan moment.

"Hello, Marshall. Lovely to see you again."

Carlotta's smile froze. This wasn't *her* fan, but Marshall's.

He smiled in recognition and rose, extending his hand. "A pleasure to see you as well, Adelaide."

She took his hand in both of hers and grinned. "Your performance at Koerner Hall this spring… Wonderful!"

As the young woman babbled on, Carlotta wrestled down a wave of jealousy that left her disappointed and deflated. And ashamed of herself. She tuned back into the conversation.

"The next time you're in town, I'd be delighted to welcome you and your—" Adelaide peered at Carlotta and clapped her hands to her ultra-bright cheeks. "Oh, my goodness. You're Carlotta Pentland. I'm so sorry I didn't recognize you, especially when you've been kind enough to come to The Stone House and allow us to feed you." Adelaide dropped a trembling hand to the back of a chair and pulled it away from the table. No sooner had her bottom touched the seat than she jumped up again. "Oh! I didn't mean to intrude. I'm so sorry." With a hasty turn, she vanished into the back regions of the diner, hands flapping the whole way.

Carlotta, Marshall, and Glory exchanged startled, amused glances.

"Temp staff. What can you do?" Glory shrugged. "In the meantime, the power-outage menu is on the specials board. Not our usual fare, but it will be hot and tasty."

After Glory left, Marshall did his best to hold in his laughter. Life on the road was hard, but priceless moments like this made it so worthwhile. He'd tease Adelaide about this the next time he dined in her family's restaurant. He could sympathize with her at his own knee-weakening moment at seeing Carlotta for the first time in decades.

A delicate snort sounded from the other side of the table. Carlotta pressed her fingers to her mouth, her eyes twinkling.

Together, they dissolved into muffled laughter. Carlotta pulled a tissue from her pocket to dab at her eyes.

Marshall took a sip of water. "Adelaide's not like that in real life at all. She's usually the perfect maître d', unruffled by the stars that go to their place. She reminds me of my daughter Serena."

Carlotta shrugged lightly. "Maybe she's upset at being stuck in town, too. I wonder why she's here." She leaned to the side so she could peek through the swing door's window. Tyler came into view. His face went from puzzled to impressed. Huh.

Marshall tapped her hand and drew her attention back to him. "I wonder why she didn't recognize you. You're just the same as you used to be."

Carlotta smiled and ignored his friendly white lie. "Probably because I don't have a huge piano beside me and I'm not wearing an evening gown."

"True. Context is everything. Adelaide and I usually meet at her family's restaurant and here I am, at a restaurant." He toyed with his knife. "Have you ever come to any of my performances?"

"No. I'm sorry." She fiddled with her fork. "My schedule never permitted it."

He laid his hand over hers; warmth rose up his arm to settle around his heart.

Glory returned, notepad at the ready. Her gaze rested for a moment on their joined hands.

Carlotta blushed, then slid her hand to her lap. To cover her fluster, she ordered a grilled chicken special with cider. Marshall ordered the same meal with a beer. She smoothed her sweater down over her waist, then captured his gaze with her own. "Why did you decide to come to Clarence Bay in the middle of winter?"

He placed the napkin across his lap. "I'd heard mixed commentary on the Festival Hall, and I wanted to look it over for myself."

She tipped her head to one side, waiting with raised eyebrows.

He shook his head ruefully. "You could always tell when I was hiding something. Okay… I hoped—wished—you would want to see me as well."

"Why?"

Marshall drummed his fingers on the table, debating his approach. "Do you remember the last time we were together?"

"In Tucson. Yes, I remember."

"We said things to each other."

Her eyes briefly lost focus as she seemed to go back to that day thirty-three years ago. "We did."

His drumming got louder. "I'd like to revisit those words."

She sat back in her chair and eyed his restless fingers.

He flattened his hand against the wood, muting his tension. "I hope to discover if our feelings are still what they were."

She crossed her arms. "Are you proposing? Again?"

As always, she was beyond blunt during moments of stress. "Not yet. After all, our memories may be more perfect than reality can hope to match."

"It hasn't even been a full day. Aren't you rushing it a bit?"

He huffed, mocking himself. "Highly likely. Just because you've been on my mind for months, doesn't mean you've given me a passing thought. I'd like us to get reacquainted, see where we go."

Glory arrived with the cider and beer.

Carlotta's look of relief at the distraction matched Marshall's annoyance. She sampled her cider, spread the paper napkin over her lap, shifted her water glass. Finally, she met his gaze. "Have you mentioned your intentions to your children?"

Not quite the response he was looking for. He sampled the beer. "In a manner of speaking. My daughter Laura is encouraging me to move on with my life. She wants me to remarry and has even introduced me to a few women. But I'll let you in on a secret…" He made a show of looking over both shoulders, "Her taste is dreadful."

She laughed, just as he'd hoped she would.

"The only woman I could think of marrying was the first woman I wanted to marry. You."

Glory came back with their meals and a side serving of avid curiosity. Carlotta frowned at gave, obviously hoping to dissuade her from gossiping. The manager her a conspiratorial wink before leaving.

They ate their meals, talking of inconsequential things. Whenever the topic turned to the past or the future, Carlotta steered them away from dangerous waters.

"What do you say, my Pearl? Shall we try again?"

Carlotta's first impulse was to say yes. Why not jump into a relationship with the only man she'd ever loved?

At that point, rational thought tapped Carlotta on her other shoulder and asked her what kind of idiot was she. She lived a perfectly lovely life and did not need to become a lonely wife of a musician always on the road. Or, heaven forbid, the faded star tagging along hoping once to again taste the dregs of glory. Her throat closed as she studied his hopeful face. She couldn't do it. Not now.

She rose abruptly and put on her coat, then bundled into her scarf, hat, and gloves. Tears pushed against her eyelids. She slung her purse over her shoulder and tucked her music case under her arm. "Thank you for lunch," she croaked. "Drive careful. Goodbye." She lifted her hand, more stop sign than wave.

She hurried from the restaurant, mopping her face with her gloves. She drove home as fast as she dared, lowered the garage door behind her car, and slipped in the side door. Once inside, she hung up her coat, exchanged her boots for sheepskin slippers, and put the kettle on the burner for tea. "Blast it all, no power." She slumped into a chair at the table. The coolness of the wood seeped through her clothing, chilling her thighs. She shivered hard. Feeling a hundred years old, she shuffled into her living room and held out her hands over to the wood stove. The stove was almost too hot to touch. "It worked! Huh." She hastened back to the kitchen, grabbed the full kettle, and set it on the woodstove. Good thing she'd read about banking the fire. Waiting for the kettle's whistle, she settled in her chair beneath the comfort of a duvet.

Thirty-three years ago, she'd met Marshall in Boston, Their chemistry had exploded, burning hotter and brighter for its brevity. The next summer, they'd met again in New York. The third and fourth summers, in San Francisco and Tucson, they'd arranged to teach in the same programs and had shared accommodations in out-of-the-way streets hidden from the prying eyes of their colleagues. They'd exchanged no promises of forever, spoken no words of love.

Only once had their schedules crossed during the following performance seasons. Heat surged through her at the memory of the little room overlooking Lac Léman on the Swiss/French border. They'd stolen a weekend out of their schedules and driven to Lausanne. That was when he'd given her the nickname Pearl. What Marshall had done with her string of pearls… She threw off the duvet, suddenly too hot.

That final meeting, ending with his rash ultimatum, had dashed hopes and shattered dreams. She hadn't seen him since, but hoarded any information about him that came her way. If she allowed herself to think about it, she hurt in the way old and deep scars pulled at tender skin. She and Marshall had shared so much and hurt each other so deeply.

And here he was again.

Still handsome, still talented, still interested.

After thirty-three lonely years. Years of hours spent at the piano, and moments of tremendous applause and glory. Years when he could have been with her. Not physically with her; that would have been impossible given their careers. But with her during the off seasons, sharing the trials and joys of global musical careers.

And here she was again.

Still with heart fluttering, still with heat flowing through her, still stupid with wanting him.

Now her career was dead, survived by recordings and radio playlists.

Now she had a more rounded life, filled with a family of friends, pupils to teach and encourage, a community where she belonged.

Still alone, but no longer lonely.

She refused to hover at the edges of someone else's glory. She refused to become a loyal supporter, sometimes manager, of star talent like other spouses. She had her pride—a pride that had seen her through the pain and heartache of walking away from her beloved piano. Her stubborn pride fed her, strengthened her. It had made her who she was. And she was not about to turn her back on herself now.

Two Days Before the Wedding

"How could you have been so horrid to Marshall," Carlotta scolded her reflection as she brushed her gray hair. "You slept like hell. No wonder you look like such a hag this morning." She tossed her brush in the bathroom drawer. "You could have just said 'no' after you'd heard what he had to say."

She was startled from her regret-filled thoughts when her landline rang. She'd given up her cell phone—a leash tethering her to a demanding career. She picked up the icy handset, a shiver rattling down her spine.

"Hello, Miss Pentland. This is Julia Westover."

Carlotta recognized the name but couldn't attach a face to it.

"I'm a singer here in town. I do ballads and blues."

"Uh…"

A sigh came down the wire. "I'm First Nations."

An image of a young and pretty indigenous woman popped into Carlotta's mind. "Oh, yes. You do wonderful renditions of the old fifty's classics. You have a lovely voice."

"Thank you."

"What can I do for you? An introduction to my agent or studio rep?"

She heard a surprised intake of breath. "While either of those would be incredible, and I'd be crazy grateful, neither is the reason I called." A long, tense silence stretched.

"Hello?" Carlotta prompted.

Julia sighed. "I know you're way, way, out of my league and my music isn't your style at all, but there's no one else in town—"

"Yes?" Carlotta prodded her to continue.

"Would you accompany me? Please?" The words rushed out, followed by a squeak.

Carlotta blinked. "Pardon me?"

"It's an outrageous request to ask a musician of your calibre to sit in the background but I'm desperate. Alex, my regular accompanist, had a gig in Toronto and he can't get back for Saturday and I *need* to do this…"

Outrageous indeed. Carlotta twisted the phone cord around her fingers. She was just about to cut into the caller's nervous babble with a curt goodbye when Julia added, "For LeeAnn."

Carlotta sat up straight, back twinging in warning. "What's LeeAnn got to do with any of this?"

"Excuse me?"

Carlotta sighed. "What does LeeAnn Hadley have to do with your request?"

"Aren't you playing during her wedding service?"

"I am."

"The disc jockey Mrs. Hadley contracted for the reception can't make it either. He's stuck in Toronto, just like Alex."

Carlotta pulled out her sternest teacher voice—the one that oddly calmed so many anxious students. "I still don't understand how this affects me, young lady."

She heard the sound of a hand drawn down a face and a deep breath. "LeeAnn's mother wants to postpone the wedding. Again. Jesper Christensen, her fiancé, wants to go ahead with it."

Carlotta huffed, thinking of LeeAnn's mother. "Good luck to him."

"Tell me about it. Anyway, long story longer, he's asked me to perform at the wedding on Saturday."

The penny finally dropped for Carlotta. "And you are without an accompanist, so you asked me?"

"Yes. Well, I didn't want to bother someone of your stardom, so I tried Asher first. But he's gone on holiday."

Carlotta growled at herself under her breath. The same pride she'd been so grateful for yesterday was now working overtime. First, she'd been offended at being asked to perform as a mere accompanist and now, she was affronted at being second choice. She shook her head. How contrary could she be? Why not help this young woman? It wasn't really an imposition; Carlotta would already be at the wedding.

"LeeAnn's crying. She's not a crier, and Jesper so wants her to be happy… and married."

"I'll do it."

A muffled squeal. "Really? Wow! I mean, that's wonderful! I'll call Reg at the Hall to book the practice room."

"I was there earlier today. Bring a sweater. See you soon."

No sooner had Carlotta hung up than her phone rang again.

"Miss Pentland, so sorry to be so brief and pushy, but I'm running out of battery." Jesper, the man of the hour himself. "Would you please change the dreadful march thing to the canon thing LeeAnn wanted?"

"Pachelbel's "Canon in D'. Certainly. It's a lovely choice."

"Bless you. Bye."

Carlotta pulled the humming handset away from her ear and stared at it. "What is going on with LeeAnn and Jesper?" Whatever the reason for the change, she would give them exactly what they deserved—the canon like it was seldom played. A satisfied smile curved her lips. LeeAnn deserved the very best.

Carlotta growled under her breath in frustration. Julia started on different beats, changed the lyrics order, altered her timing, all on a whim. It was like she used the sheet music as suggestion rather than specific instruction. How did Julia's regular accompanist do it?

Carlotta didn't want to hurt the singer's feelings, but she had to say something. Once, in Italy, a careless concierge had left her stranded. She'd tried to catch a cab, but they all ignored her. The only Italian she knew was musical direction—*allegro, espressivo, con pedale*—useless in day-to-day conversation. She'd wandered the streets, trying to find a way to the venue until a friendly expat had helped her out.

That was how she felt now, familiar with the landscape and yet stranded. The actual music was no problem at all, but she just couldn't predict Julia's improv. "Julia, is it possible to choose a plan and stick to it?"

"What do you mean?"

Julia's shoulders drooped. "We've both learned something today. Shall we take a break? Get a coffee or something?"

"Or maybe a litre of wine?" Carlotta suggested with a wry smile.

Julia chuckled and nodded.

Resigned, Carlotta rose from the bench. A small twinge in her lower back reminded her to stretch. She hated that she couldn't get into the swing of Julia's music.

Julia had confessed, that she didn't have formal music training. It was like they were speaking different languages.

But Carlotta knew an excellent musical translator. If she dared to contact him.

Contacting Marshall was easier said than done. How did one man disappear from a locked-in, snowed-under, frozen-over town?

She knocked on Reg's door and entered when he prompted. He rose from his desk chair, pushing aside a pile of glossy flyers as he did. He strode around his desk with a huge smile. "What can I do for you, Ms. Pentland? I'm sorry the room isn't warmer, but we're conserving fuel. Who knows how long the power outage will last? A few hours or…"

"Not to worry. The room is fine. Julia and I are both wearing enough layers to keep us warm."

"It's the noise from the main hall, isn't it?" he asked, continuing to fuss on her behalf. "I can't believe how many people have shown up. At least, they're generating their own heat."

"No, it's not that. I'm looking for Marshall Rickerts. Do you know where he's staying?"

His brows lifted, wrinkling his forehead. "Are you sure, miss?"

"Very sure. Do you have the name of his hotel?" Never had it been so difficult to ask for a serving of humble pie.

"No, miss. He didn't say, and I didn't ask. However, I do have his cell number from our negotiations. Would that be of use to you?" He lifted his phone, then paused, flicked a glance at her, and turned away from her view.

Carlotta rolled her eyes. Reg was a lovely man, but he was rather punctilious. "Yes, please." Borrowing a pen and sticky note from his desk, she jotted down the number he read out. "May I use your office phone, please?"

"Of course." He moved from behind his desk and gestured for her to take his seat, then sat in his guest chair to listen in.

Maybe she should think about getting a cell phone again. She had to nudge him with raised eyebrows and a pointed look at his door. At last, he got the hint, made an exaggerated gesture of taking papers from his desk, and left. Carlotta sighed, got up, and closed the door behind him. Huh, she'd never noticed the bathroom, with tub and all, hidden behind the modern panelling. Time for a little procrastination with a quick brush of her hair.

It took Carlotta several tries to pick up the receiver. Her hand shook so badly, it took three tries to hit the correct buttons and several more tries before she got the call to go through. Only, after three rings, it went to voice mail.

For a moment, her heart sank. He must be so angry at her that he was refusing her call. Then logic kicked in. The call display would show "Reg Barker" or possibly "Festival Hall". Assuming Marshall would pick up for Reg, she concluded his phone must be out of service. After all, places to recharge one's cell were few and far between at the moment.

She tried the front desk of the Dungannon Motel, one of the few places in town open in the winter. Marshall, the concierge informed her, was keeping warm by the fire in the lounge with the other guests. Did she wish to speak with him? Good question. Would she rather apologize to him and ask her favour over the phone or in person?

She owed him a heartfelt apology for her careless dismissal. And now, she desperately needed him. Jesper was relying on her and Julia to entertain their guests.

The concierge cleared his throat, forcing a decision. She declined the transfer and returned to the practice room.

"Well?" Julia ceased pacing and turned to Carlotta.

"Do you think Marshall Rickerts would be of any help?" Carlotta said.

Julia's smile lit up. "Wouldn't it be wonderful if he happened to wander by?" Her shoulders drooped. "We can dream, right?"

"Well, actually…" Carlotta said.

Julia straightened, eyes narrowed. "Are you telling me Marshall Rickerts of the Quâtre Jazz Quartet is in town this very minute?" At Carlotta's nod, Julia threw her hands up and did a happy dance. "Why didn't you say so?"

Carlotta's cheeks burned.

"So, he's stuck here." Julia grinned, lifting her hands to the sky. "Thank you, polar vortex!" She hustled over to where their coats were piled on a chair, snatched up her red parka, jammed her arms in the sleeves, and sprinted through the open doorway.

Carlotta went to the piano and packed up her music, then Julia's. By the time she was done, Julia was back, wearing a bemused look. "Aren't you coming?"

Carlotta couldn't hold in her laughter, even if it did come with a nervous edge. "Yes. I'm just not quite as hasty as you are." Carrying the two music cases, she strolled over and donned her own navy coat.

Julia blushed when Carlotta returned her case to her. "Sheesh, crazy fan moment or what?"

"Indeed," Carlotta teased her new friend.

Outside, it was warmer than earlier this morning, a bit above freezing. Carlotta and Julia debated over whose vehicle to take. Julia had more gas, so in they got and off they went.

"I should've asked earlier… do you know Marshall?" Julia asked as they left the Hall parking lot.

"I did. Back in the day. We met at several summer programs over the years." And one unforgettable weekend in Switzerland. Heat rushed up Carlotta's chest and flowed over her face. She yanked off her white beret.

Julia glanced over at the gesture. "How well did you know him?"

"A little. Not very well." She unwrapped her blue scarf.

Julia laughed. "Hot flash? From menopause or Marshall?"

It was a toss-up, but Carlotta kept that to herself. "When do you think the power will come on?"

Julia twinkled at her and allowed the change of subject. They chatted about the weather for the rest of the brief trip.

When they arrived, Carlotta turned to Julia. "I lied earlier. Marshall and I knew each other very well back in the day. He came to town earlier and I was… not very nice to him." What a gigantic understatement. "Would you mind waiting in the lobby for a few minutes? I need to apologize to him first."

Julia's eyebrows rose. "Wow. Um… okay… no worries." She gestured towards an upholstered bench between a couple of large plants. "I'll just wait over here. Come get me when you're ready."

Carlotta touched Julia's arm briefly. "Thank you. I hope it won't be too long." *And that she'd actually get to meet him.*

Pausing at the archway into the Dungannon's lounge, Carlotta scanned the rustic wood-panelled room. Muted light flowed over groups of chintz-covered chairs. A wood stove against a rock wall radiated heat. An unlit Christmas tree looked forlorn in one corner.

Marshall rose from a seat by the picture window. He dropped a magazine to the table beside him.

Carlotta smiled sheepishly and moved towards him.

"You're still here."

"I didn't have much choice." The ice in his voice rivalled the frost on the windows.

She couldn't blame him, though, after her chicken-hearted dash from The Pits. She cleared her throat to loosen the tension. "The polar vortex is messing up the roads, trapping people everywhere."

"You're here to discuss the road conditions?"

"No." She flexed her fingers in the calming ritual she'd always used before a performance. "I came because I—" *Need you? Want you?*

Frigid silence.

"I came because… I want to apologize. I was horrible to you in the restaurant. You were nothing but sweet, and I just ran off."

He crossed his arms. "Why did you do that?"

"I…" She stretched her fingers again. "I… umm…" She dropped her chin.

"I promise not to bite." His voice was a wee bit gentler.

Staring at the red and brown swirly carpet, she swallowed hard and pushed the words out. "I don't want to become a hanger-on, following you around on tour, making arrangements. I couldn't stand to hear the whispers. 'She used to be a star, you know. Look at her now. A shame. So sad.'" She drew a deep breath. "I'm sorry I wasn't honest with you." She walked over to the window, staring out at clouds laden with more snow and shivered, even though she still wore her coat.

His muffled footsteps followed her. Even as anxious as she was, his nearness calmed her.

"I'm sorry, too." he murmured in her ear. "I'm sorry you didn't stay to hear me out." With a gentle tug on her arm, he turned her to face him.

She still couldn't look him in the eye. Such a nice tweedy blue sweater he wore.

"I retired from performing a few seasons ago and have managed the quartet since. But I'm done with that at the end of next season. It's a huge relief to lay down the burden of a perfect performance."

Her mouth dropped open, and she finally raised her eyes to connect with his. "But… you're at the peak of your career!" Alarms screeched in her head, making her gasp. "You don't have health issues, do you?"

He shook his head. "No health issues, but I'd say the peak happened a few years ago. I took a page out of your book and quit while the quitting was good." He clasped her trembling hands. "Now I want to start something new, or rather, restart something old and cherished. I hope."

They smiled at each other, heat and hope blossoming between them.

"Are you done yet? Did you ask him yet?"

Marshall was surprised to see beautiful young woman approach them. She froze the moment she laid eyes on him. Her dark eyes widened, and her hand rose to her chest. Call him a vain peacock, but he still got a thrill from these moments of recognition. And this was the second time in this small town. Who knew?

He glanced at Carlotta. She was watching the reaction of her friend, sharing in the moment.

Carlotta gestured to her friend. "Julia, meet Marshall Rickerts. Marshall, this is Julia Westover."

"Pleased to meet you, Julia." He held out his hand. She reverently placed her hand in his.

"Mr. Rickerts, I'm so pleased to meet you. I'm such a huge fan. I have all of your recordings." She laughed awkwardly. "I'm trying so hard not to squeal the place down."

"Call me Marshall. What is Carlotta supposed to have asked me?"

Julia took back her hand and cradled it, acting as if she'd never wash it again. "I've never met such a Big Name before." Her eyes rounding in horror, she turned to Carlotta. "Oh my gosh, except you, of course. Oh, my God, what have I done? I'm so sorry. I'm always sticking my foot in my mouth. Please don't give up on this. Please forgive me."

The poor girl babbled on until Carlotta laid a hand on her arm. "Don't make yourself sick about it. Now, hush." She turned to him and said, "You recall I'm playing at a wedding on Saturday?"

"Yes," he said.

"Well, people are trapped—much like you're stuck here— and neither Julia's accompanist nor the expected DJ can make it. So Julia has asked me to accompany her."

"But…what's that to do with me?" he said.

"Julia is a crooner. She sings Sinatra-style. As that's hardly my forte and Julia is…" She struggled for a nice way to say frustrating to work with, "…very improvisational, which is also not my forte—" She broke off.

He nodded. "Ah, I see. You do have a problem."

Carlotta gave him a wry twisted smile.

"Why not postpone the wedding until things are back to normal? Is there a need for such a rush?" he said.

Carlotta threw a questioning glance at Julia who replied with a shrug. "Neither of us are aware of a need to hurry to the altar. However, LeeAnn, the bride, means a lot to us."

Had Carlotta simply apologized to accomplish a hidden agenda? He frowned at that disturbing thought, then set it aside for when they were alone. "What's so special about LeeAnn, that you would both go to such extreme lengths for her."

While Carlotta gathered her thoughts, Julia spoke up. "I've been friends with LeeAnn since high school. She stood up for me a few times, sat with me when other kids ignored me. Supported me in my choice to sing 1950's music…" She grimaced. "LeeAnn came home with me, to the reserve, to talk to my grandfather. He'd rather I sang only our traditional songs. Lee-Ann even started a dance group, arranged for a teacher to come up from Toronto once a month. I sing for them; the gig got me other gigs, spread my name a bit. And now LeeAnn is getting married—or trying to—to the guy she should have married three years ago."

"Should have married? Explain, please."

"LeeAnn and Jesper got engaged about three years ago—before you came, Carlotta. I've never seen two people so fly-me-to-the-moon happy. The whole town was thrilled for them. She's a teacher at the primary school. All the kids love her, so do all the parents. She gives her time everywhere, helps out any way she can. She's always so kind and so cheerful. Anyway, they'd made all their arrangements, and she asked me to sing. I couldn't wait to pay her back for her generosity. But then her dad had a massive stroke and died a week before the ceremony. Everything was cancelled."

Marshall and Carlotta made sympathetic sounds. Carlotta hadn't known about this before.

"LeeAnn and her fiancé Jesper started making arrangements again this summer. But this time, LeeAnn's mother took over. I was not invited to sing this time. It seems Sinatra isn't classy enough for the likes of Mrs. Hadley."

Marshall was beginning to fill in the blanks. "And now the power outage has shut everything down and freezing rain is on the way and…"

"Jesper called. LeeAnn is so upset at cancelling again, she's actually shouting at her mother, and crying, and… She's beside herself. So, I'm doing what I can because I owe LeeAnn."

"LeeAnn sounds like a gem." He smiled at Carlotta. "What about you, Pearl? Do you owe her as well?"

"Yes, I do. When I first arrived here, I was reluctant to get involved with anyone in town. Honestly, I didn't know how to make friends. I'd forgotten, or possibly never learned." Was that another price she'd paid for her career? "I became a bitter recluse, dealing with back pain and the loss of my identity."

She'd never talked to anyone about her life-altering decision, and now here she was, talking to the same person twice in two days. Her agent had ranted and raved about lost revenue, loss of stature, etc., etc. But they never spoke of the physical and mental pain. Marshall understood the loss. He'd been with her at the peak of her performance—still young enough to blaze with passion for the music—before the passion got buried beneath the job of performer.

"You're a strong and brave woman, Carlotta."

She lifted her gaze from her twisting fingers. No, he wasn't ridiculing her. He wouldn't.

"But there was one person… LeeAnn understands the importance of music to youngsters. She convinced me…" Carlotta chuckled. "More like begged, cajoled, pleaded with me to teach musical basics to the children. She promoted the class... and even badgered the parents for extra funding."

"LeeAnn sounds like a force to be reckoned with."

"She is indeed. I predict she'll run for public office someday."

"So LeeAnn arranged for you to teach a children's introduction to music class. Lucky kids."

"No, lucky me. Because she didn't stop there. She found parents who would pay for private lessons. I met Asher through her. That was his piece you heard me playing at the Hall. LeeAnn got her Aunt Louise, the flower shop owner, to introduce me to the Chamber of Commerce, and they asked me to join. Louise was my first true friend in Clarence Bay. And she connected me with other friends."

"It must have been an awkward fit to start with...a world-class pianist and a bunch of small-town folks."

"I have to admit that was my first thought, Marshall. I was such a snob," Carlotta said with a tight, shame-faced smile. "I'm not sure why LeeAnn persisted, but I'm so glad she did."

"She saw you as a person rather than a talent." He hung sarcastic quotes around the last word.

Carlotta absorbed the idea. "You're right. That's exactly what she did. To LeeAnn, I'm a person first and a pianist second. She opened her heart to me and brought me into her life. She calls me her favourite auntie." Carlotta pressed her palms to her heart, tears gathering in her eyes. "I owe her more than I can repay. My life in this town is a real life, with good friends and a community, a place where I belong for the first time in my life."

"Though some people call you Miss Pentland," Marshall said.

"That's what I get for being so stuck-up when I first moved here."

Julia wrapped her arm around Carlotta. "No. We call you that from affection now."

Marshall interrupted their friendly hug. "You still haven't said where *I* come into this."

"LeeAnn's fiancé wants to give her a surprise wedding and I—we—want to help him achieve that." Carlotta laid a hand on his arm. "Will you please help me and Julia, so Jesper can marry his LeeAnn?"

Marshall covered her hand with his. "Of course. Good thing I never travel without my clarinet."

THE DAY BEFORE THE WEDDING

"Good morning, Pearl," Marshall said, clipping his seatbelt on. "Another frosty one, eh?" Even the quick dash from the hotel lobby to Carlotta's toasty warm car had him shivering. He still couldn't reconcile the timing of her apology and her request for help. He'd slept fitfully, struggling with the idea that Carlotta was manipulating him for LeeAnn's benefit. Today he would push for an answer. "I assume Julia is waiting for us somewhere?" he said to Carlotta as they drove the short distance to the Hall.

"She should be in the practice room by now. It doesn't have the awesome acoustics of the auditorium, but the Hall is open as an emergency shelter, so a crowd has taken over that space."

Marshall escorted Carlotta through the Hall's imposing glass doors, taking off his hat and gloves as he entered the main auditorium where people sat about chatting and drinking hot beverages. Children ran around in a raucous game of tag. A few people hunched over cell phones and other devices; they must have found ways to charge up. But not here. A sign posted rules; no recharging allowed; a landline is available in the office for emergency use only. Chatter, laughter, and the noise of life fill the Hall.

Marshall clomped along in his heavy boots, following Carlotta as she moved through the crowd, frequently stopping to chat, laugh, share, and socialize. At one time, she would have hustled through a crowd like this, shy and hunched over. More likely, she would have found an alternate route through a building. Now, she was a cherished part of this small northern community.

He barely recognized her.

The thought stopped him in his mental tracks. Was she the same person he'd loved with such passion all those years ago? Had he come on a fool's errand after all?

"Excuse me, mister." A young boy scooted past him, his posse hard on his heels. Marshall spotted some family likenesses in a horde of younger children chasing after the first group.

At last, he and Carlotta made it to the rehearsal room. As he shut the door behind him, the noise diminished to a dull roar thanks to the soundproofing. Julia, who was studying sheet music at the piano, turned to them.

Marshall laid his clarinet case on the piano, tossed his parka and scarf on a chair, and rubbed his hands together. "What have you got?" he asked gesturing to the music laying on the piano. Julia handed him the stack. Turning the pages, he recognized familiar tunes from the golden era of swing, big band, and blues. The tunes made famous by the Rat Pack featured largely.

"Nice selection. Is this your repertoire?"

"Not all of it. Just the pieces I thought LeeAnn would like best and that might work for a wedding." Julia blushed and straightened defensively. "I haven't had a lot of training, but the people around here like what I do."

Marshall groaned to himself. What had Carlotta gotten him into? He smiled at the nervous young singer. "Always a good start. We'll run through the lineup and see what we get. Carlotta, please have a seat and warm up." Marshall withdrew his clarinet, popped the reed in his mouth to prepare it while he assembled his instrument. He played piano and several woodwinds, but clarinet was his true love and the one he took with him wherever he went.

Julia watched, agog with fan glow.

Marshall smiled to himself. The young woman had forgotten her role in the proceedings. "Julia, do you have a warmup routine?"

She started out of her trance. "Oh, yeah. I did it while I was waiting."

"So, let's hear what we can do."

They started with the song Julia selected for LeeAnn and Jesper's first dance. Marshall could never hear *that* song without thinking of pearls shimmering in moonlight streaming across a rumpled bed. He exchanged a long look with Carlotta.

Her face glowed rosily as she gave him a secretive smile. She remembered.

Julia's lack of training didn't make any difference to her voice. She had two and a half octaves at her command with a surprising ease at the lower end. Her breathing gave her away, though. She tried to make her too-shallow breaths last too long. Marshall worked with Julia, teaching her techniques to manage her breath, when to sneak in sips of air to lengthen her notes.

Carlotta was having a terrible time with the unfamiliar jazz rhythms underlying the music. She'd never cared for jazz, so she wasn't lying when she said she couldn't feel the music. Yet she struggled on.

Undaunted, he sat at the piano with Carlotta. Heat bloomed down the side of his body nearest her.

"Accompanying a singer is a different skill than playing solo. A soloist is a star. When playing with an orchestra, the orchestra bows to the soloist. Similarly, an accompanist must bow to the singer."

Carlotta stiffened. "It's been a while, but I remember all that stuff. I just can't make it happen." She bounced her fists on her thighs.

He nudged her shoulder with his. "Your skill as a soloist is beyond compare as is your knowledge of the classics."

She grimaced. "In jazz and blues, not so much. Is that what you're saying?"

He smiled to soften the blow. Soloists generally had somewhat neurotic egos from years of front-line exposure. "Yes."

"Okay," she huffed. "Show me how to do this."

"Julia, from the top." He played the intro bars, gave her a nod to begin. As he listened, he learned her way with the music, her rhythm and phrasing. He followed her, supported her, strengthened her performance. As he played, he spoke to Carlotta, seated on the bench beside him, attempting to distill his years of experience into quick tips.

Carlotta listened carefully, despite his warm breath against her ear. After a couple of times through, she took back the keyboard, observing Julia. Gradually, Carlotta grew comfortable with her musical conversation with the jazz singer.

Marshall stood and lifted his clarinet to his mouth. He gazed down the length of black wood, setting fingers to keys and air holes. He flicked the reed with the tip of his tongue and snuggled the mouthpiece between his lips.

Carlotta's hands stilled in mid-air over her own set of keys. She stared as desire spread from her belly to her legs. Her mouth went dry; she licked her lips.

He gave her a conductor's glance to begin the piece.

She didn't acknowledge the instruction, just kept staring at him while lust bubbled through her blood.

He gave a slow, mischievous wink, a pronounced twinkle in his eyes.

Heat stung her cheeks. She peered under the piano to find the correct pedal, straightened her back, lifted her hands, and gave him the long-awaited nod.

Julia chuckled through the introductory bars and smiled through the opening phrase. She added a swing to her hips and shoulders as she settled into the song's message.

For the first time, Carlotta understood the appeal of these old ballads. Heartbreak and joy filled their lyrics. Slow syncopated rhythms seduced listeners to hurry up and relax; time was on their side.

Marshall's music shuttled between Carlotta's steady baseline and Julia's melody, weaving magic, stitching music and voice together with skill and patience.

During the long afternoon hours, as the light dimmed, Carlotta's ease with Marshall grew steadily. Memories rose, especially the one featuring her pearls. All these years later, heat still flowed through her belly and her body still clenched.

Glowing with triumph, Carlotta rose, pressed her palms to her lower back below her waistband, and twisted her torso in a stretch her physiotherapist had taught her.

"I'm sorry, Pearl. Was it too much for you?" Marshall asked. Julia hovered as well, worry pinching her features.

Carlotta rolled her shoulders one way, then the other. "I'm a little stiff, not in pain. Nothing a hot bath and time in bed won't fix."

Julia uttered a tiny gasp. Marshall fought a grin.

Too late, Carlotta spotted the alternate meaning in her own words. Carlotta's face flamed. She opened her mouth to scold him as she would have done back in the day when she was all music, all the time. But a scold wasn't in her. For the first time in years, she'd had fun making music with other musicians.

"You two are very naughty people." She wagged a playful finger and laughed aloud. A burden shifted, and her soul lightened.

Marshall broke down and cleaned his instrument before tucking it into its cushioned case. "Can I take you two lovely ladies to dinner? If Cherrystones is still open."

"Thanks, but I've already got plans." Julia said as she gathered her sheet music and tapped it into a tidy stack before storing it in her backpack. "See you at the wedding, tomorrow, four PM sharp. Then she grabbed her coat and raced out of the room.

The decisive snaps of the closures on Marshall's clarinet case echoed in the sudden silence.

Shyness clamped down on Carlotta. She rubbed her hands together in a washing motion. A large hand stilled her agitation. Lifting her head, her gaze met Marshall's warmth.

"You were wonderful today," he said.

Her mouth opened to brush off the praise, to list every error she'd made.

He pressed a finger to her lips, stalling the words. "Perfection is no longer required. You've paid your dues. Your professional days are done. Now your job is to bring joy to others and yourself."

She blinked up at him as the truth rolled through her. She was done with the burden of perfection. Her soul gave itself a good shake. "Thank you for reminding me."

"You're welcome." His hand fell to his side. "There's something else I want to remind you of. I had a question about our relationship… but I don't want you to answer just yet." He looked toward the windows for the view of a frozen bay. All he got was a reflection of themselves in an empty room. Prophetic of an empty future? "Your apology yesterday was… Let's say, unfortunately timed."

Carlotta hung her head.

"Did you attempt to manipulate me with the timing?"

She shook her head. "No. I realized I owed you a couple of apologies before Julia called for help. Her request made me question myself and my pride. I would have saved us both some hurt if I hadn't gone with my knee-jerk response to your words. Let me ask you something. Did you assume that I was easily available now that I'd retired?"

"No." He paused and looked away. A sudden guilty flush filled his face. "Okay, yes. I wasn't looking forward to a lonely retirement. I looked back on our past and longed for what we'd shared. Without giving it much thought, I assumed you might feel the same way. I'm sorry. It was an appalling assumption."

"I did recall the past, but obviously, not the same way you did. The ultimatum you gave me to curtail my career in favour of yours—was never far from my mind. So I immediately assumed you were talking about the same thing."

"The only sameness I was looking for was the special togetherness we shared. How we could argue over the smallest thing and end up laughing like loons. Our appreciation of the same things." He gave her a sly wink. "The way we played with pearls."

Heat flooded her body. She grabbed his forearms with the intention of pushing him away. Only her hands had other ideas. They slid from his arms, wrapped around his waist, and pulled him closer until his chest and hips aligned with hers.

He slid his arms around her, completing the double circle, then kissed her, pressing his body against hers. And she revelled in it, settling in like a cat in front of a fire. She never wanted it to end.

Gently, he set her from him. "Will you come back to my hotel? We'll stop at Cherrystones for takeout, if they have it."

She shook her head, then smiled at the devastation in his eyes.

"If you're anything like me, you've had more hotel time than you can stand. Would you rather come home with me? I have a banked fire in my wood stove and lots of blankets. We can stop at The Pits for takeout."

His face broke into joy. "I would love to go home with you."

A few minutes later, as they peered in through the darkened windows of the Pits, they couldn't see anyone, nor were there any lights in the apartment above. Huh.

"Guess they lost their backup power," Carlotta said.

Beside her, Marshall straightened away from the glass. "So, no food for us. Now what?"

She pulled him towards the car. "How does soup and grilled cheese sandwiches made on a woodstove sound? With tea or coffee? Or extra chilled white wine?"

He pressed her back against the car for a quick kiss. "As long as I'm with you, that's all that matters."

She laughed at his gallantry and slung her arms around his neck to return his kiss. A stiff breeze slid icy fingers down their collars, reminding them they had a warmer place to go.

Once there, they pushed open her front door, and a surprising warmth greeted them. Carlotta stirred up the embers and stoked the fire from the pile nearby. "Banking the fire kept my house warm—well, warmish—all day. And there are enough embers left to jump-start a new fire."

"Speaking of fire…" Marshall walked over and hugged her from behind, nuzzling into the side of her neck. She murmured her approval and tipped her head. For long minutes in front of the cozy fire, the popping and snapping of the flames provided melody to the lyrics of love. Carlotta drew Marshall down the hall to her bedroom; clothes slipping, lips sliding, bodies reaching… and, finally, blankets pulled snug against the chill.

THE WEDDING DAY IS HERE

The next morning, Carlotta was so hot when she awoke, she threw back the covers without bothering to open her eyes. Menopause was a bitch.

"G'morning, Pearl, my love."

Carlotta shrieked and yanked the covers back up over her nakedness. Sure, they'd spent the night together, but love handles, no matter how small, were meant to be hidden.

Marshall chuckled and rolled closer... then immediately rolled away. "Damn, you're burning hot!"

Her blush compounded the heat of her hot flash. "It's par for the course for an old besom like me."

"Old besom like that woman we met in France? Not on your life." He rose on one elbow and propped his head in his hand. With his other hand, he traced lazy circles on her bare skin, easing the covers down with each circle. The Christmas Spirit, was listening, leading them back to a lost love. How could it be coincidence? If not for a bride he'd never met, he'd likely have waited out this miserable deep freeze and gone home empty-handed and empty-hearted. "I love you, my Pearl. Will you marry me?"

"I love you, too. Of course, I'll marry you." She reached for him, and he came to her.

Joyfully.

Hours later, they hurried downstairs to stoke up the fire and cook up a late brunch. Sated in front of the fire, Carlotta tossed off the afghan and rose from the couch. "Now let's go play for our supper."

Snowbound Feast

Stormy Wedding 3

Four Days Before the Wedding

Adelaide Somerset wanted food, so she turned off the highway at the next intersection. But she wanted real food from a real restaurant, so she let the golden arches slide past, as well as other fast-food joints. She noted where the gas station was for her return trip. Food first, gas later.

As she drove, she looked out the windows of her car. Nice little town. Hmm, smoked fish and meat looked promising, but at almost eight o'clock in the evening, the place was closed. Ditto, the bakery, promising but closed.

She spied a mom-and-pop place, Cherrystone's. Could be a bust... A voracious growl from her stomach made the decision. An icy wind rushed up her skirt as she slid down from her Lexus SUV and she pulled the fur-trimmed hood of her down coat over her head. Good grief, it was cold.

Christmas wreaths hung in the window. She pulled open the door of the restaurant; family-friendly, cozy, battered, super clean. Her restauranteur's training kicked in as she waved back to the brawny barkeep-slash-bouncer-in-need. Informal. A dozen square wooden tables with a wild assortment of wooden chairs. Six beat up stools at the bar. Not the least threat to her family's restaurant The Stone House. Adelaide pulled her thoughts up short. She sounded like her father, judging every food service business like he was a TV star. *Think positive, not Dad.*

She found a table away from the darkened chilly window, not too close to the other patrons, but close enough to the swinging door where she might catch a glimpse of the heart of the place—the kitchen. A couple lingered over dessert and coffee; relaxed and happy, clearly taking their time and enjoying themselves.

A woman appeared with a friendly smile. "Hi, welcome to Cherrystones on this frosty evening. My name is Glory and I'll be your server tonight." She placed a glass of water above the utensil roll and laid a menu and a liquor list in front of Adelaide. "Tonight's specials are cream of leek and potato soup and linguine with clams."

Adelaide returned the smile. "What do you recommend?"

"Do you want a light meal or something to fill you up?" She pulled out a notepad ready to take the order.

"Something to fill me up."

"Any allergies or sensitivities?"

"None."

Glory tapped her pen on her pad, clearly giving Adelaide's wishes some thought.

Anticipation rose in Adelaide.

"Grilled cheese?"

Oh. Her shoulders dropped. In her mind, she could hear her father's rant about low class food. *Shut up, Dad.*

Glory's smile twisted to one side. "Yeah, I know. I doubted, too, but Chef pulls it off. Give it a try."

Adelaide's stomach growled, saying yes before her mouth could say no. She pressed a palm to her midsection.

The server grinned. "May I suggest a cider to go with it? We have non-alcoholic if you're driving."

"You've convinced me… Grilled cheese with sweet cider."

Glory picked up the menus and pushed through the swinging door. Adelaide leaned forward for a quick peek into the familiar domain. A tall man, wearing a black denim bib apron over a white t-shirt and blue jeans, lifted his focus from the grill to respond to Glory. Beneath a checked chef's beanie, an open smile lit his handsome face.

Oh, my. That smile appealed to the deepest wishes of her heart for sweet unconditional love.

He peered past Glory through the swing door's porthole.

Adelaide thrust herself back into her chair. She should have stuck her nose into her book instead of peering through the kitchen door.

The door swung open, and she got another glimpse of the handsome man in a cook's apron. She'd love to linger over coffee and get to know him. But she had an appointment with her father in Toronto tomorrow morning. An appointment where she would ask, again, to be named to the position of pâtissier. And Dad would, again, turn her down. Argh. What would it take for Dad and his brothers to see her value on the team? That her skills were wasted in her current position of maître d'.

For now, her grilled cheese sandwich arrived. "I dare you not to love it," Glory said.

Adelaide's eyebrows rose at the challenge. She examined her food; the bread, artisanal white; the cheese, far from plastic. She picked up the fistful of food and sniffed. *Mmm.* The smell made her taste buds pay attention. She took a bite and chewed, savouring the crusty bread and soft cheese. Her eyes drifted closed. Flavours burst in sequence, mild cheese, sharp smoky cheese, mushrooms, tomatoes, and…sage. A groan escaped her.

"Told you."

Adelaide opened her eyes, expecting to see a smug-faced waitress. Glory smiled like she'd shared the world's best secret. Adelaide dabbed at her mouth with her napkin. "You are correct. This is incredible. My compliments to the cook. He has a marvellous way with a sandwich."

"I'll tell Chef. My guy is top-notch." She nodded and moved to another table to pick up a ticket.

Her guy. The words implied the cook was her husband, though he seemed a bit young for Glory. An unexpected shaft of pure green envy rose inside of her. She blew out a breath to release it. Whatever. All she cared about was good food.

And this was seriously good food. The sandwich and sweet cider were a fabulous combination, and Adelaide planned to enjoy every bite. Along with every peek she could get at the cook, wife notwithstanding.

Adelaide was deep into a novel on her e-reader when Glory came to remove the empty plate. "*Crème d'érable* for dessert? Coffee or tea?"

"*Crème d'érable?*"

"It's like *crème caramel*, but with local maple syrup."

"Sounds divine. Yes, please. With coffee. If the crème is anywhere near as delicious as the sandwich, I will be one satisfied customer."

Glory nodded and smiled, happy with Adelaide's agreement.

Adelaide wondered why it was important to her make the server, and therefore the cook, happy. And that was no ordinary cook back there, that was a man with mad skills.

As she finished off her cider, the couple across the room got up to leave. The guy went to the back and knocked on the kitchen door. The cook peered through the porthole and came into the front of the house. The guys gave each a man-hug, and the woman got a kiss on the cheek.

Like a voyeur, Adelaide watched the interaction between the three friends. The others were pretty people, but they didn't draw her attention like the cook did. His eyes crinkled with laughter at something his friend said. Tall and strong, the cook gave the impression he'd be up for anything.

Her pulse fluttered. It had been so long… she missed intimacy with a man. Dare she take a chance on just one night? Was he open to taking that chance with her?

The woman raised her left hand and a diamond sparkled. The couple were engaged.

Another shot of envy hit Adelaide square in the heart. Her eyes filled with tears. Embarrassed, she snatched her napkin off her lap and dabbed at the moisture.

"That good, eh?"

Adelaide started.

The cook stood at her table. She gaped up at him, shocked by the blue of his eyes and their teasing glint. His open smile compounded the shock of… recognition?

Tyler leaned over the chair tucked under the table. "Are you okay?" he asked the customer dressed in tall boots, short skirt, and sleek sweater. His fingers twitched to tangle in her long chestnut hair.

She blinked her dark eyes up at him, looking a little stunned.

Tyler empathized. The same stunned sensation sizzled along his spine. "The *crème d'érable* is tasty enough to make you weep with joy?"

Her gaze followed his gesture to the plate in front of her. Her head tipped to one side as if she were puzzling out where the food had come from. She pressed her hands to her flaming face, hiding her deep dimples. What the heck was she thinking?

"I—um—uh—yes, it's delicious. Are you the cook who made it?"

Should he be flattered by her stuttering or insulted by her question? When in doubt, he'd go for the positive. Life, as he knew from way-too-close experience, could be over in a moment. And this moment was too good to pass up. "Thank you. Yes, I did make it. I'm the chef here at Cherrystones." No need to tell her the locals called it The Pits.

Her distinction between chef and cook bugged him. A chef had training to back their talent. A cook had talent, usually undeveloped, and perhaps some solid self-taught skill going for them. He'd been trained at a recognized college—business basics, front of house, back of house, the works. He was a chef.

She nodded, accepting his declaration and everything it meant.

She also licked her spoon… Blanking his mind to all around him.

"What did you put in the crème, other than maple syrup? A warm spice, atypical for custard." She scooped up another mouthful, her attention focused on her taste buds. "Not cinnamon, nutmeg, or cloves. Allspice?"

He gave her a chance to show off. At least, that's how he excused his silence.

She took another spoonful.

Could he become that spoon in that mouth?

Her eyes shut as she rolled the custard over her tongue.

Hot erotic images filled his mind's eye. Licking crème off her bare breast, her belly, her—

"Cardamom," she crowed. "It's cardamom, isn't it?"

"Uh…." He shook off his stupor. "Yes. You're the only person to get it right."

"What's my prize?" A tiny smile, a suggestion of seduction, was all the invitation he needed.

"A kiss. Your prize is a kiss."

"From the chef?" Her gaze wandered over his body, head to toe, with a slight pause just below the knot in his apron strings.

A quick scan of the room confirmed they were now alone; customers were gone, the staff had left for home. He'd told Glory he would deal with this last bill. He extended his hand. Without breaking eye contact, she placed her hand in his— queen to his courtier. Geez, he'd gone a little nuts in his imagination. She rose, forcing him to step back, placed her other hand on his shoulder. Standing just close enough for him to feel her heat, to swoon in her sophisticated scent.

He lifted her hand to his lips and kissed the back, the skin fine and thin over the bones and tendons. He gave her a tiny wink. It had been so long since his last relationship. Dare he take that chance with her?

She returned a sexy pout and slid her fingers from his clasp though she didn't let go. Instead, she turned his hand up, flicked her tongue in the centre of his palm, and dropped a soft kiss on the slight dampness.

He damn near exploded. Heat surfed up his arm, down his chest and arrived in his crotch on a tsunami of lust.

She lifted her face, eyes teasing, lips puckered and demanded her payment.

Happy to be outmaneuvered, he gave in to her invitation and lowered his head.

Soft, pliant, inviting. Her kiss drove everything from his mind… except the need to have her naked with him.

He pulled back a step. Her eyes dared him, double-dog dared him, to come back. He grinned; her smile deepened her dimples to creases. She shared his enthusiasm. "Will you stay?"

She nodded. "Yes, please." Her wicked smile belied her demure response.

He grasped her shoulders. "Stay put. I'll be right back." Moving fast enough to leave a breeze in his wake, he locked the front doors and flipped the sign to *Closed*. He dropped the blinds and pushed in a couple of crooked chairs. Racing through the kitchen he flipped the deadbolt on the back door, thrust a bowl of eggs in the fridge, and stowed his knives. By the time he was back, she'd picked up her coat and purse.

"Are you Glory's husband?"

His eyes rounded. "No way. Uh… she's a terrific person and all, but I'm nobody's husband, fiancé, boyfriend or significant other. I'm all yours."

"Excellent." She sighed in relief and raised her hand, palm up. "Take me where you want to go."

Grabbing her outstretched hand, he led her through the tables and down the hallway separating the restaurant from his private quarters upstairs. He stopped at the row of light switches, and with a practiced sweep of his forearm, he plunged the entire first floor into darkness. Only a light at the top of the stairs showed the way to his apartment. Happiness lit her face as she followed him every step of the way.

Several hours later, Adelaide woke up. It took her a few moments to recall where she was and why. Hmm, yes. A one-night stand with an amazing lover and chef. Which came first in awesomeness, his cooking or his loving? Such a delicious conundrum. She giggled to herself.

Beside her, he stirred and rolled over. When he reached for her, she went to him. His hot naked skin and burgeoning erection tempted her to stay.

"I have to go. I have a morning appointment in the city." She gave him a lingering kiss. "You're a wonderful lover. Thank you."

"You're kinda wonderful yourself. I'm sorry you can't stay. I make a mean midnight waffle."

"As tempting as that is…" She let the sentence trail away as she got up and got dressed.

He pulled on jeans and a sweatshirt and slid into his kitchen clogs, then grabbed up a coat and escorted her through the dark quiet front of house to the street door, and all the way to her car down the street. Cold air swirled up her skirt—her tights did little to keep out the icy bite—and she shivered.

Hunched into his jacket, he held the door for her.

"Goodbye, Angel. Come back soon."

"Goodbye, Chef." Reason as cold as the air made her hesitate to commit to returning. Adelaide settled for one last lingering kiss, then got into her car. The gas gauge hovered on empty; she'd have to stop at the gas station at the edge of town. The car clock read 11:28 PM. By 2:00 AM, she'd be snug in her condo. As she passed through the traffic light, the streetlights flickered. There was a split second's worry before the lights steadied.

Relieved, Adelaide drew up to the gas pump and climbed out, into the bitter cold. Scurrying around the end of her car, she unscrewed the gas cap and inserted the nozzle, turned and waited for the gauges to clear.

The overhead lights flickered again and steadied. She squeezed the trigger, and the power went out. She groaned and waited for the power to come back. She stared at the black faces of the gauges, giving the trigger another futile squeeze. A nasty wind blasted against her thinly clad legs and a shiver racked her body. She slammed the nozzle back in the holder and shut her gas tank. Crap! She didn't even get a drop of gas. Pulling her coat tight, she ran, almost wiping out on an ice patch before she made it inside.

A young man in his late teens sat behind the counter, his thumbs flying over the tiny keys of his phone.

Adelaide waited in the dim light coming from the emergency lighting on the wall behind him. Out of patience, she knocked loudly on the counter. "Excuse me."

The kid jumped and his phone clattered to the glass. "Hey!" He snatched up his phone and checked for mortal injuries before giving her his scowling attention.

"The pump stopped working." She pointed outside.

"Yeah. No power, no pump, no gas."

She was irritated at his tone of voice, but she had bigger problems. "Okay. Is there a station in town where the pumps are working?"

"Uh… lemme check with my friend at the other station that's open this late." He hunched over his phone.

She wandered up and down the aisles, found her favourite chocolate bar on sale, two for $2.49. Yes. Sometimes a woman needed her chocolate.

Back at the counter, she calculated the sales tax in her head and counted out the exact change. She plunked the chocolate bars and cash on the counter as the teen finished his texting.

"No luck. Power's out all over town and beyond."

Her shoulders slumped. She ripped open a bar and bit off a chunk, thinking as she chewed. "Is there someplace in town I can stay overnight?"

"Uh… a motel on James Street is open all winter. The rooms will be stupid cold cuz they don't turn on the heat until somebody shows up."

"Any other place?"

He shook his head and shrugged. "Not unless you know someone in town."

Her body hollered to her; she knew someone with a snuggly warm bed. Unfortunately, she didn't know either his last name, or his first name, to call him. And she refused to ask the kid.

"I can call my mom. She'd probably let you bunk in with my little sister."

"That's sweet, but I don't want to intrude so late at night." She sighed and her shoulders slumped further. "Guess it's the hotel. At least it's better than sleeping in the back seat of my car. Would you give me directions, please?"

The teen pulled a free map off the display and drew the route she should follow. She thanked him and left. Huddled in her coat, she pointed her car back towards town. Turning right, she recognized the street where Chef lived. How she longed to stop. She forced herself to aim the car straight down the road, praying she had enough gas.

Suddenly, her car sputtered, gasped, and died. Chimes from the dashboard told her the obvious. The tank was empty, with not even fumes to run on. She fought the steering wheel to pull over to the side of the road—right in front of Cherrystones.

The sight of the restaurant filled her with heat... and memories of seeing that man in an apron—and out of it—filled her mind.

But the place was dark. He was probably zonked out in his warm bed. *Duh. Of course, it's dark—there's a power outage.* But still, it had been simply a no-names, one-night stand. That was all.

Sighing, she reached behind her to wrestle her small leather duffle bag into the front seat. If she was going on a long march through the cold dark streets of town, she needed more layers of clothes. As she zipped open the bag, a light came on in the kitchen of the restaurant. The yellow beam shot through the porthole, a golden path flowing across the floor, through the front door, and into her eyes.

She had a decision to make—an embarrassing reunion with an intimate stranger or a cold dark march in the middle of winter to wherever.

Decisions, decisions.

She zipped her bag shut and lugged it, her purse, and her laptop across the street. Huddled in the minimal shelter of the recessed doorway, she lifted her hand to knock. This was going to be so embarrassing. A frosty breeze chilled the thought. Better embarrassed than dead.

She knocked.

No response.

Grimacing, she knocked louder and longer.

Chef's surprised face appeared in the kitchen door's porthole.

She waved and cracked a hesitant smile.

Seconds later, she was enveloped in warmth. And shivering so hard she could barely stand. Her teeth clacked, her knees knocked, her bones rattled.

Chef opened his arms and drew her close. The shiver transferred to him. "Damn, you are one cold cookie." He led her upstairs to his warm, messy bed. It would have been so romantic— if she hadn't been shaking so bad. He removed her clothes, tucked her under the covers, got naked, and climbed in beside her, then drew her back to his bare chest and tucked his knees behind hers.

Several long minutes later, her shivers subsided, and she fell into deep and dreamless sleep.

Three Days Before the Wedding

Tyler woke to sunlight streaming through his window and across his side of the bed. Beside him lay the beautiful woman he'd spent a few blazing hours with last night. She'd left and he'd never expected to see her again. And yet, here she was, naked and in his bed. He wasn't quite sure why but thanked his lucky coin. He grinned and reached for her.

She purred and stretched under his stroking hand. Her eyes popped open and showed a moment's confusion.

She blinked and smiled, then held out her hand. "Good morning. My name is Adelaide Somerset and I'm pleased to meet you."

He shook her hand. "Good morning, Adelaide. My name is Tyler Hadley and I'm delighted you stopped by. And even more glad you came back." He leaned over for a brief hello kiss. "Why did you come back?"

"I was low on gas, so I stopped at the station. The power went out as I squeezed the trigger. The cashier told me how to find a motel, but it looks like the Christmas Spirit had other plans." She stroked her fingertips against his rough whiskers.

"I see. *The Christmas Spirit* decided you were meant to be in my bed?" He trailed a fingertip over the curve of her breast.

"Well, okay, *I* decided." She arched into his touch, prompting him to toy with her eager nipple. Her breath caught and she clasped his erection. There were no further words for another hour or so, only soft moans, whispered encouragements, and satisfied sighs.

Tyler slapped a hand on the alarm clock, fumbling for the off button. He'd just woken up—for the second time—and rolled over to confirm he hadn't dreamed a night of wild anonymous sex followed by a morning of wild acquainted sex.

Nope. Adelaide was still here, sound asleep on the other side of the bed. Her straight chestnut hair spread across the covers and over the pillow.

He slid out of bed and dressed without disturbing his snoozing beauty. Downstairs, he flipped on the lights and started to prepare bacon and sausages, mixed pancake and waffle batters, and sliced challah for French toast while visions of Adelaide danced in his head.

Just before Glory was due to arrive, she called him. "I forgot my keys. Can you open the front door and let us in?"

"Us?" he asked. But she'd hung up.

At the front door, the usual breakfast group had morphed into a crowd of epic proportions.

"Start taking orders," Glory barked at him as she headed through the kitchen door to hang up her gear. "I'll call the other staff to come in."

The crowd flowed through the doors and spread out across the tables. Quicker than he could say "What the waffle?", the restaurant was full.

At table five sat the Gossiping Grishams, feeders and keepers of the Clarence Bay grapevine. "Thank God you've got a generator," Melody said as she shed her bright blue, down-filled parka.

"We do? I mean, we do, but why are you so thankful?"

All three Grishams stared at him with popping eyes. A major coup; silencing all three of them at once was a rare feat in the town of 6,500 souls.

"Don't you know there's a massive power failure? The whole town is dark," Melody said.

A vague memory of the lights flickering and the generator kicking in late last night floated up. That was minutes before Adelaide had come back, shaking with cold. His face stung with heat at the not-so-vague memories of what had followed her return. "Guess I was in bed."

Significant glances flashed between the Grishams, sly smiles slid from one to the next, some of those smiles sliding over his shoulder. Without turning, he knew who stood behind him. And now the town's gossip royalty had a very good idea why he hadn't noticed a minor detail like a town-wide power outage.

A soft hand crept into the crook of his elbow. Adelaide stood beside him, wearing tight jeans and his Clarence Bay hockey jersey over a turtleneck sweater.

"Can I help, Tyler?" Adelaide asked.

He turned to her and clasped her hands. "Can you wait tables or cook?"

Her gaze slid away to tour the room. "Yes, I can wait tables and do some cooking, though baking is my specialty."

"Let's talk to Glory, the manager." He escorted her back to the kitchen.

Adelaide scanned the rectangular room. A beat-up bar table and three stools were squashed into the corner beside her. To her right, a counter held a prep area, a six-burner stove and grill, and a serving area. A glass-fronted cooler filled with drinks and a huge commercial fridge occupied the left-hand wall. Opposite her, an exterior door crowded the sink and dishwasher. In the far corner, a staircase led to the basement. There was only enough room for a brigade of chef and dishwasher. It was a long way from the full brigade in her father's kitchen… with no room for another pâtissier.

A frustrated Glory slammed down the phone by the table. "Damn, most of 'em are no shows."

"I found help," Tyler said.

Glory gave Adelaide an assessing up and down. Her eyes flicked back to him a couple of times. "Can you wait tables, do a plate, flip a burger? Or just eat?"

"Yes," Adelaide squared her shoulders. "All of the above."

The exterior door banged open. "I made it!" An older teen sagged against the counter. "Damn, it's frickin' freezin' out." She unwrapped the many rounds of her scarf and headed to the lockers. She paused in front of the group. "New staff?" she asked Glory.

"Temporary. We're slammed with extra covers because of the power outage."

"Okay."

"Glad you're here, Jessie. The dishes will be piling up soon, so step lively." Glory tossed Adelaide a white waist apron and a book of tickets. "Get rockin', girl!"

At ten, when only a few tables lingered, Glory declared a morning break. She made two mugs of coffee and plunked them down on the battered bar table in the kitchen. "Take a load off."

Adelaide slumped on the second stool Glory pointed at. The delicious scent of well-made coffee was balm to Adelaide's fatigue. It had been a long time since she served tables; she'd forgotten how physically punishing it could be.

Glory tucked a strawberry-blond curl behind her ear. "Glad the morning rush is over. I hope the folks still out there won't camp overnight." She added cream to her mug and took a satisfied sip. "Thank God for generators, eh?"

"Generators?" Adelaide peered over her lifted mug.

"Uh…" Glory stared at her. "City girl, are you?"

"Yep. Got a problem with that?" Adelaide tipped her head, too tired to huff.

"No, not at all. What do you do when the power goes out?"

"Uh… wait for it to come back on?"

"What if it's out for days on end?"

"Oh, like the summer when I was a kid? The whole Eastern seaboard went dark. Yeah, we just waited for it to come back."

"Up here in cottage country, some of us have standby generators to supply emergency electricity when the power goes out." Glory cocked her head, listening. "You hear that rumbling noise?"

Adelaide stilled, tuning in to the noises beneath the sounds of running water as Tyler cleaned the grill and tidied up. "The noise that sounds like a truck?"

"Yep. That's a generator. It uses gas like a truck but makes electricity instead of turning wheels."

Adelaide stared up at the lights, heard the radio in the background, watched Tyler put eggs back in the fridge. "Huh. I thought the power was back on."

"Only in this building," Glory said.

"So that's why so many people are still hanging around? They don't have generators?"

"Some will have fireplaces to warm them. But if they haven't got a gas stove, they can't cook. So here they are."

"And here they stay," Tyler said as he dropped onto the third stool and set down his laden plate. "Lucky, I got my delivery yesterday, so we have plenty of food."

"How long do power failures last around here?"

"Not long. Couple, three days."

"Two or three days? Is that all?" Adelaide mocked his cool acceptance.

"They're getting worse as the infrastructure ages."

"It's a crime the way the power company ignores its responsibility for maintenance," Glory said.

"More and more generators are getting installed," Tyler said.

"Why don't the gas stations have generators?" Adelaide asked.

"Corporate couldn't care less about small towns."

Adelaide turned to Glory. "That's why I'm still here. The gas station was down. I was on my way to the motel, but the car ran out of gas right across the street, so…." She shrugged.

"It was fate," Glory finished for her.

Adelaide glanced at Tyler. He sat with his mug halfway to his mouth, an arrested expression on his face. A secretive smile pulled at the corners of his mouth and lit the depths of his grey eyes. He nodded and raised his mug in a salute.

A blush burned her cheeks as she returned his smile.

"Did it just heat up in here?" Across the table, Glory fanned herself. "Guess you two found a room, eh?" She chortled at her own joke, then got up to clear her place at the table. "Carry on."

"Don't mind her," Tyler reassured Adelaide. "This whole town is nuts about gossiping, especially if it involves anything the least bit romantic."

"You mean people will gossip about me and you and…?" Adelaide pointed overhead towards the bedroom.

"Yep."

She shrugged. "Doesn't matter. I won't be here for long." Funny how much it hurt to say those words. "My father expects me back ASAP."

The smile slid from Tyler's face, leaving a tight frown. "You called about your appointment with him?"

"Yeah. He was not a happy man." The rant was the latest in a long line of rants about her failure to meet his expectations. What about her expectations of him? Hmm…

Tyler said nothing, just scooped up the dirty dishes and headed for the sink.

Still preoccupied with her question, Adelaide headed to the swing door. She paused, grinned hugely, and dashed out of the kitchen and over to an older couple being seated by Glory. She bumped into Glory and muttered a quick apology. "Hello, Marshall. Lovely to see you again."

Recognition in his smile, Marshall stood, extending his hand. "A pleasure to see you as well, Adelaide."

She took his hand in both of hers and beamed at him. "Your performance at Koerner Hall this spring... Wonderful! What a coincidence that we're both stuck in the same town. I ran out of gas and Tyler was kind enough to offer me shelter. The next time you're in town, I'd be delighted to welcome you and your—" she looked over at his companion and clapped her hands to her nuclear-hot cheeks. "Oh, my goodness! You're Carlotta Pentland. I'm so sorry I didn't recognize you, especially when you've been kind enough to come to The Stone House and allow us to feed you." Adelaide drew back a chair with a nervous hand. No sooner had her butt touched down than she jumped up. "Oh! I didn't mean to intrude. I'm so sorry." She sprinted into the kitchen, flopped down at the table, and buried her red face in her folded arms. "Great time for a fangirl moment! Argh! So embarrassing!"

Glory swung through moments later. "You work at The Stone House?"

"What did you say?" Tyler's footsteps approached.

Glory crossed her arms. "Surely, you've heard of The Stone House, Tyler."

He huffed in disbelief. "Who hasn't? Everyone I know who's ever eaten there raves about it."

"Our girl here, our skilled temp staff, works at The Stone House."

"Wow. Is that true, Adelaide?" Tyler asked her.

Glory snapped her fingers and pointed at Adelaide as if she were a celebrity. "You're one of *those* Somersets, aren't you?"

"Yeah." Adelaide nodded, embarrassed again, but for a different reason.

Tyler's eyes widened. "Seriously? You own The Stone House?"

"Not me. My family owns it. My dad is executive chef, and my uncle is *chef de cuisine*."

"And you're the *sous chef*?" Tyler said it like it was a foregone conclusion.

"Nope. *Maître d'hôtel*." Just the *maître d'*. Yes, it was a responsible and influential position, but… she wanted to bake. Pushing up from the stool, she squared her shoulders and walked over to the prep station. "Now, haven't we got some work to do for the lunch crowd?"

Two Days Before the Wedding

"Good morning, Tyler. How are you this grey and blustery day?" Glory swept into the kitchen on a blast of icy air.

Sunny side up, over easy, and done hard. Tyler smirked as he cracked eggs into a bowl. "I'm fine." Better than fine. "How's the town holding up?"

"People are doubling up in houses with generators that are still working. I wonder if there's some way we can set up a monster generator for the whole town?" She stared off into space for a moment. "It's something to ask the mayor about. Anyway, where's Adelaide?"

"Rolling silverware and setting tables," Adelaide replied as she swung through the door and hopped onto a stool. "Can you point me to the S&P? Shakers need filling."

Tyler's phone rang, and he tugged it from his apron pocket. "Hey, Jesper. How ya doin'?" He leaned his elbows on the counter.

"Do you have power?" Jesper asked.

Tyler's brows drew together at his friend's brusque tone. "Yep. Do you still have power?"

"Yeah, we're good." A long, harsh sigh came over the connection. "Listen, Tyler, I hope this isn't too much to handle, but I need you to do our reception on Saturday."

Tyler jerked upright in surprise. "You what? What happened to the fancy-ass caterers Norah ordered?"

"The highway's closed because of this damn storm. We have no caterers and no cake."

"No caterers! Shit." From the corner of his eye, he saw Adelaide and Glory snap bolt upright on their stools. Big ears, the pair of them.

"Tell me about it," Jesper groaned.

"The obvious solution is to postpone the wedding, right?"

"Yeah. I know." He heard heavy footsteps pacing over creaking floors. "That's what Norah wants." Jesper ground his teeth. "LeeAnn can see the logic but—" He swallowed hard. "Listen. She's shouting at her mom and crying her eyes out." Jesper choked on his emotions. He loved his fiancée with his entire being. "LeeAnn's your cousin and I know there's something important between you two, though she's never said, and I trust you...."

Tyler fought his own battle with emotion. Time to out the truth. "She saved my life. If not for her, I'd be nothing but a long-ago smear on the railway tracks."

Adelaide and Glory echoed Jesper's gasp.

Tyler was still pretty horrified himself whenever he thought of The Incident.

"Tell me," Jesper demanded.

"Gimme a sec." Tyler drew a calming breath as he went to sit beside Adelaide. For some weird reason, he needed her by his side. "You remember how, when we were all kids, Shelby always followed us around."

Jesper chuckled. "She was a major pest."

"One Saturday when I was sixteen, LeeAnn and her family came over for a barbeque. Me, being your average family-averse teenager, took off for a walk. And Shelby, being a pesky kid sister, followed me. I wanted to put a toonie on the tracks to see if the pieces would come apart."

"Cool… Did it work?"

Tyler pulled his lucky coin from his pocket and laid it on the table. Adelaide and Glory stared at it with popping eyes. The two-dollar coin was slightly curved and a lot elongated. The Queen's profile was squashed and distorted. But the bronze centre held strong in its silver ring.

"I'll show you the next time we get together."

"So what happened?" a twitchy Adelaide insisted.

"Who's that?" Jesper asked.

"Adelaide Somerset." He glanced at her. How to describe her, other than someone who'd very quickly become very special to him. "A new friend."

"Okay." Jesper waited for Tyler to continue.

"Anyway, I was at the tracks near the trestle over the marina, the coin was in place, but no train came. I got bored, so I started walking a rail like a tightrope."

"Tell me you weren't stupid enough to go on the trestle," Glory said with her hands at her throat.

"Not quite that stupid. Like I said, I was walking the rail. I'd gone to the trestle and was headed back. Shelby thought it would be cute to scare me, so she rushed through the bushes, growling like a bear."

Jesper laughed. "Some bear."

"It wouldn't have been a problem except at the exact same second a train blew its horn from the far side of the trestle. Both things together startled the hell out of me, and I slipped off the rail, twisted my ankle, and hit my head so hard I passed out."

"God."

"Yeah. He, or a guardian angel, was definitely involved in what came next." Tyler choked up.

Adelaide put her hand over his white-knuckled fist. He grabbed her fingers and held on tight.

"I was unconscious, so I only know this next bit because Shelby told me. The little misery tried to haul me off the tracks, but I was too heavy for her to manage alone." After all these years, his heart still seized at the image of a skinny little girl trying to move an almost-grown man while a screeching train barrelled down on the pair of them. "At the last possible minute, LeeAnn jumped on the tracks and dragged me out of the way of a nasty death."

Tyler's jaw clamped tight. Adelaide stood and hugged him sideways. He leaned into her, drawing strength and comfort.

"How did LeeAnn get there?"

"She had a strong feeling she should follow Shelby. That Shelby might get hurt and need some help."

"Wow, no wonder LeeAnn never fails to follow her instincts," Jesper said over the phone.

"They didn't fail her that day. Or me."

"Damn it, man, I'm fucking glad she was there for you."

"Me, too." Tyler glanced from Adelaide to Glory. Both wore their mixed emotions on their faces: shock, horror, gratitude, tears.

He tapped his lucky coin, making it rock on its curved back. He snapped one side with precise pressure, and it flipped, rocking on its edges to show off its distorted polar bear. Tyler snapped again, and it flipped again. "In conclusion, I will do anything I can to make LeeAnn happy. Except bake a cake. Sorry."

"All righty then. No cake, no worries. My mom should be able to do something."

Adelaide pounded his shoulder.

"Yeah?" He turned to her.

"I can bake a wedding cake."

"By Saturday? Today's Thursday."

"I *am* a pâtissier. I *will* make a wedding cake."

"What is she saying, Ty?" an impatient Jesper asked.

"Well, Jesper, the Christmas Spirit is looking out for you two as well. A pastry chef happens to be stuck in Clarence Bay for the duration, so LeeAnn will have her wedding cake."

Adelaide snatched Tyler's phone from his hand. "Hi, Jesper, Adelaide here. Can you give me any details about the wedding cake to help me replicate it?"

A surprised silence was the only reply. Then… "Uh, hi, Adelaide. Nice to meet you. Uh, I'm Jesper Christensen."

"Yes, you're the groom. Tell me about the cake that was ordered."

"Uh…. I don't know anything about it. All I was told was what to wear and when to show up. Norah, my mother-in-law-to-be, ordered it. LeeAnn didn't want it."

A groom who didn't know anything… Wait! "The bride didn't want a wedding cake?"

"She hates fruitcake."

Adelaide blinked in shock. "Then why…," She waved away the puzzle. "Never mind. What did LeeAnn want instead of fruitcake?"

"She wanted a bunch of cakes, pies, and pastries, like a… a dessert buffet. Why?"

"What are her favourite flavours?"

"Chocolate, raspberries, cherries, lemon... anything maple."

A good man knew his love's preferences. "Allergies?"

"None. Why do you keep asking?"

She stroked Tyler's arm; so glad he was there, and that Lee-Ann had trusted her instincts. "After what we just learned, I want to give LeeAnn whatever she wants, too."

More silence, then finally. "Okay."

"How many servings were planned?"

"One hundred was ordered, though I haven't a clue how many people will be there. How ever many are sheltering at the Festival Hall? None? More than a hundred?"

"Okay, thanks."

"No, thank you for helping out a perfect stranger. Pass me back to Tyler, please."

Her mind spinning with ideas, she did as Jesper asked.

Tyler put his cell to his ear. "What's up?"

"You can take all the meat you need from our store. I think there's some duck *confit* ready to go. Leeann will love that instead of the boring chicken stuff Norah ordered." With a smile in his voice, Jesper rattled off the door's combination.

"That'll help. We've still got power here, so we'll do everything we can for LeeAnn's feast. It should be easy with your top-quality food."

"Thanks a lot, Tyler." Jesper hung up with a gruff goodbye.

Adelaide came in for a crushing hug. Glory doubled it.

Adelaide straightened and scrubbed the wetness off her cheeks. "Take me to your pantry," she demanded. Grinning, Tyler led her down a short hall to a cool dark room lined with rows of shelves laden with dry goods. Giant bags of rice and pasta filled one shelf. Potatoes, onions, garlic, and shallots occupied more space. Standard cake-making ingredients—flour, sugar, leaveners, basic spices, chocolate, and gallons of maple syrup had a dedicated shelf. The freezer held bags of frozen summer fruit.

"Score!" She pumped a fist. "I foresee chocolate ganache in my immediate future." Everything she needed went on a wheeled cart. "How many eggs have you got? How much milk? Any whipping cream?"

Tyler led the way back to the kitchen and over to the walk-in fridge. Inside, she found eight dozen eggs, lots of milk, several industrial-sized jugs of whipping cream. Thank goodness The Pits had received a delivery yesterday. They stopped at the equipment locker for every baking pan and tray Tyler didn't need. They had piping equipment? It all went on the cart as well and up the stairs to Tyler's standard kitchen with its one barely used stove and one nearly empty fridge.

Adelaide spread out her treasure trove, opened her laptop and started scanning her private file of recipes… chocolate ruffle cakes, raspberry almond cardinal slices, *clafoutis*, *crêpes Suzette sans alcool*, macarons filled with cherry whip. And of course, she'd get the awesome *crème d'érable* recipe from Tyler. She had two days to put it all together. Talk about a bake-off challenge!

Downstairs, four dozen hand-raised *tourtiéres* lined the counter, ready to go in the oven when the *cassoulet* came out in a few minutes. The *confit* would be crisped in a hot oven at the Hall. None of this was on the menu at The Pits, but LeeAnn had fallen in love with French-Canadian cuisine on a trip to Quebec City with Jesper. Tyler had developed the recipes just for her and cooked them whenever she asked.

He stood at the grill, dry roasting an assortment of vegetables to go into as many serving dishes as he could find.

Glory had decreed a restricted menu of sandwiches to let Tyler and Adelaide put together LeeAnn and Jesper's feast. She now breezed in, built five plates of sandwiches and potato chips, poured coffee, put it all on a tray, and vanished. Jessie followed and did the same.

Tyler spared a thought or three for Adelaide, upstairs in the tiny kitchen of his flat. She'd run off with vast quantities of cake ingredients and spices. She'd gone nuts over the frozen fruit. How was she managing with one standard oven?

The generator hummed outside.

Adelaide swung through the door. "How's it going down here, Tyler? I'm waiting for things to cool before the next step."

Speaking of an angel… "So far, so good," Tyler called over his shoulder as he tossed precision-sliced celery into the heap of fennel and shallots sizzling on the grill. "Can you see a bowl of mushrooms somewhere?"

She placed a huge metal bowl of perfectly cut mushrooms on the counter beside him. "Here you are."

"Thanks." He added them to the other vegetables, where they soaked up every drop of juice and oil. Given how long the power had been off, and the number of people he'd heard had gathered at the Hall, the quantity would have to go around the block more than a couple of times.

A drop of water sizzled on the grill.

Where had that come from? He checked over his shoulder. Adelaide was tidying the kitchen for him. What a sweetheart. Glory and Jessie were both out front.

Another drop hissed on contact with the hot metal.

Tyler looked up.

A few more drops came through a crack in the fireproof ceiling tiles.

"Oh, crap." The words dragged out of him.

"What's wrong?" Adelaide asked from across the room.

Tyler pointed up at the drips turning into a thin trickle. "We've sprung a leak."

Adelaide came to his side and looked up as well. "Uh, oh. Not a good thing." She cupped her hands under the trickle; they filled in a moment.

Before Tyler could respond, the ceiling tiles sagged. As they stood gaping, the tiles split, and a waterfall splashed down onto the hot grill, sizzling and spitting in all directions.

Tyler thrust out an arm to push Adelaide back as he stepped away from danger.

A cloud of steam rose from the hot mess of vegetables. Seconds later, the fire alarm started screeching.

The grill cooled as more water poured from the gap in the ceiling, splashing them both on the way to the floor. Vegetables went with the flow, slopping onto the white ceramic floor.

Dumbfounded, Tyler turned off the gas.

Glory and Jessie slammed through the door and shrieked. People crowded behind them.

Snapping back to himself, Tyler turned and ran for the basement stairs, slipping on the greasy vegetables sluicing towards the floor drain. Pain stabbed at his lower back as he regained his balance. On the way down the stairs, he clocked himself a nasty one on the overhead beam at the bottom. Bright flashes of light slashed across his vision. Grabbing his head and groaning, he staggered over to the power panel, and slammed down on the main control lever.

Idiot move. Now he couldn't see in the hellish gloom.

He groped for the flashlight on top of the panel. Clicking on the powerful beam, he turned and tripped over an empty bucket, landing hard on one knee. Whimpering from the pain, he rose and kicked the bucket clear across the basement. It clanged against the metal storage units. Was this his own personal re-make of "Home Alone"?

He paused to gather his bearings. The next lifeline to cut off was the gas main, then the water main.

The sound of shouting filtered down the stairs. Clutching the flashlight with one hand and his sore head with the other, he ducked below the beam and limped up the stairs.

Utter chaos filled his kitchen.

No one noticed his arrival over the sound of water still flowing through the ceiling. Thank God, it had now turned into a trickle. People shouted and laughed and made stupid suggestions. His piercing whistle muffled the crowd. He limped around the mess formerly known as a wedding feast.

"Okay, everybody, the party's over. Finish your meal and go on home, or to the Hall, or wherever you can find shelter. The Pits is closed, your meal is on the house."

Everyone stood and stared at him.

Adelaide stroked his forehead. Her fingers were cool against his skin. His eyes closed at the soothing touch.

"Poor Tyler. That's a heck of a goose egg you got there, for sure."

Glory smothered a laugh in the back of her throat. "You heard the man." She herded everyone out of the kitchen.

Tyler groaned as he sat on the stool and cradled his aching head in the palm of his hand.

Adelaide slid the flashlight from his grip, snapped it off, and laid it on the table. She walked between his spread knees and wrapped her arms around him. He leaned into her soft strength and breathed in her sweet scent. How was it possible for one man to hurt all over, be soothed all over, and be horny all over, all at the same time?

They stayed that way until Glory came back. "The house is empty. Let's get this mess cleaned up."

Tyler lifted his head.

Adelaide dropped her arms and stepped back, missing Tyler's heat and weight, the way he trusted her to care for him. She stared at the mess. Water dribbled from the ceiling. Oil, water, and veggies slimed the floor. Half the *tourtiéres* were a sodden shame. Was the filling salvageable enough to make stew?

When Tyler tried to stand up, Adelaide pressed him back onto his seat. He looked awful, pale and disheartened. "You stay put," she said.

"Can't." He tried to stand up again.

This time, Glory put her hand on his other shoulder. Adelaide exchanged a smile with her, and they both pressed down.

"Stay put. We'll clean up. You think of how we're going to finish a wedding reception dinner without a kitchen."

His chin dropped and he stared at the mess, rubbing his bruised knee.

"Mop? Squeegee? Stuff like that?" Adelaide asked Glory.

Glory opened a cupboard in the corner. She handed a floor squeegee to Adelaide and lifted a large bucket. "I'll go next door and get some hot water."

Adelaide glanced at Tyler slouched on his stool. Poor guy. She pushed the mess over the floor drain to get rid of the oil and water. In the cupboard, she found a dustpan and shovelled the ruined food into the compost bin. By then, Tyler had crossed his arms on the table and laid his head down. Dark shadows under his closed eyes and a big purple bruise on his forehead stood out against his pale skin.

"What's left in your friend's store?"

"A whole lamb," he said without opening his eyes. "You don't happen to know how to butcher a lamb or roast it whole?"

She placed some painkillers and a glass of water on the table. "When I was a kid, our Greek neighbours roasted a whole lamb in their backyard every Easter." She shrugged. "That's all I know. Sorry." She put away the squeegee. "Does this Hall place have a kitchen?"

He straightened and gaped at her as if someone had conked him with his own frying pan.

"Are people being fed or is the Hall only for shelter like a warming centre?" she asked.

"Uh." He swallowed the pills. "Thanks."

"If food is served at the Hall, where does the food come from?"

"Uh."

She tipped her head and smiled at him. "You don't know, do you?"

He grinned back at her and reached for his phone. "But I can find out."

Glory returned with a bucket of hot soapy water and Adelaide helped her mop the floor and wipe down the grill. By the time everything was shiny clean, Tyler was off the phone.

"There's no food service at the Hall, though they do have a full commercial kitchen for banquets and wedding receptions." He hopped off the stool, wincing when he put weight on his knee. "So let's grab what we can and head down to the Hall."

"Sounds like an awesome party, but I have to go home to my kids as soon as we've got you loaded," Glory said. "Sebastien's had enough of watching his little sister."

Thirty minutes later, Adelaide waved goodbye to Glory, then turned back into the darkened restaurant.

Adelaide gazed around the Hall, amazed at the open space, noisy and crowded with people of all ages. Soft grey light flowed in through enormous windows looking out over a frozen bay. A conga line of children, led by a tall teen girl with sandy curls, snaked around piles of cots and groups of adults. The teen waved as the giggly chain step-kicked past her and Tyler. The wave flowed down the line. Adelaide grinned and waved back. Muted music filtered into the space from somewhere close by.

A tall, balding man with a walrus moustache entered from a side room. Music poured out and was silenced when he closed the door with exaggerated delicacy. He strutted about the Hall, scanning arrangements and issuing orders when something didn't appear to suit him. He gave a regal nod to Tyler and a sharp-eyed up-and-down glance at Adelaide.

"Who's the Master of Ceremonies?" Adelaide asked Tyler.

Tyler looked up from tapping on his phone and laughed. "That's Reg Barker, the general manager of the Festival Hall. He's very proud of *his* Hall. Crazy crowd, eh?"

"This is the crowd we have to feed?" She stretched her arms wide. "We certainly didn't bring enough food with us. Where will we find more food? What about drinks? Is the kitchen big enough? Is there any staff? Good grief!" Her voice climbed higher.

He waggled his phone. "No worries, sweetheart. I have a plan. Texts are on their way as we speak." He gave her a wry smile. "Here's hoping all the phones in town aren't dead."

"Tyler! You're here!" A vaguely familiar thirty-something woman grabbed his arm to turn him around.

He lurched on his weak knee. "Hey, Mel." He gave her a warm smile.

"Yipes!" The cute blond placed a hand over her heart. "What happened to your gorgeous face? And did your knee just give out on you?"

Adelaide slipped her hand into Tyler's warm grip. Mine. Adelaide frowned at the possessive thought. What was she thinking, claiming a man she'd only met two days ago? A man she'd slept with for two nights and had awesome sex with many times. A man who was now stroking his thumb down the back of her hand, soothing her thoughts.

"I had a close encounter with a beam and a bucket in the dark," he told the woman.

"You poor thing. The perils of a blackout. Do you need an ice pack or some painkillers?"

Tyler tipped his head toward Adelaide. "All taken care of."

The woman's speculative gaze lingered on their clasped hands, then moved from Tyler's face to Adelaide's. She gave a sly wink, as if to say she'd keep Adelaide's secret.

What secret that was, Adelaide had no clue. It was impossible she had fallen in love with Tyler, wasn't it? It was far too soon.

But what about last night…?

The blond tapped his arm. "Introduce us, Ty."

"Bossy much?" he protested.

"Not at all. Just doing my job…" She waved a small notebook. "…the old-fashioned way with pen and paper."

"Adelaide, meet Melody Grisham, writer of the gossip column for the local newspaper. *Beware the Grishams*," he said with a teasing overtone of warning.

She wagged a scolding finger at him. "Mock in haste, repent at your leisure. Our research shows that you, and everyone else in town, read my column before you read anything else in the paper, hardcopy or online."

Adelaide wondered how many people heard the hurt and resentment in Melody's voice. Familiarity bred contempt. Adelaide knew all about it.

"Melody, this is Adelaide Somerset, stranded visitor and baker extraordinaire," Tyler said.

Adelaide couldn't help but preen a bit as she extended her hand. "I stopped in town for food and fuel, had a lovely meal at Cherrystone's, then got caught at the gas station with an almost-empty tank at the very second the power went out. I was on my way to a motel when I ran out of gas outside Cherrystone's. Tyler kindly offered me shelter." *What is it about this perfect stranger that makes me want to blab my story?*

Melody returned the handshake, her curious gaze probing Adelaide's secrets once more.

"Did you hear about LeeAnn's and Jesper's wedding?" Tyler asked Melody.

And now Tyler is telling all. Melody is definitely in the right career.

"I assumed they cancelled it because of the power outage." She jammed her fists on her hips and her eyes narrowed. "What do *you* know that *I* don't?"

"Jesper still wants to have a wedding for LeeAnn. He's got Shelby doing flowers and Julia doing music. Adelaide and I are taking care of the food."

"Why in the name of all that's worth hearing, is he doing that now? In the middle of a massive power failure? Is the man nuts?"

"Yep. Nuts in love." He cocked his head. "Got a problem with that?"

Adelaide's mouth twitched at his sly misdirection.

Melody reared back, mouth open, eyes flicking between them. She was silent for a minute, thinking. She shrugged. "Well, all righty then. How can I help?"

"We've got a lot of stuff in the truck that needs carrying into the kitchen and trucks full of food on the way."

"Really?!" Melody stabbed a finger over her shoulder toward the big man instructing people how to precisely rearrange the tables. "How did you talk Reg into letting you use his precious kitchen? He wouldn't let any of us near it."

"It's been booked for months for LeeAnn's wedding, so he's holding it for us."

She flapped her arms. "Well, that's Reg for you, the expert *official.*"

"Ty, I got a message you need help. What's up?" A bearded guy in a red plaid shirt came up to them.

"I got one, too," said another guy and another and another.

"I can help in the kitchen," said the sandy-haired teen. "My Nana Jean taught me how to bake." A mom with a kid on her hip also volunteered. More responses echoed around the room. Soon, they had more help than they knew what to do with.

"I'll make a list of duties," Tyler said.

"And I'll make a list of volunteers and their skills. Then we can match them up." Adelaide suggested. "Melody, can you spare your pen and paper?" Turning to the crowd, she hollered, "If everyone could form groups. Kitchen helpers over the double doors, decorator helpers by that plant…"

"Tyler!" Reg Barker interrupted, hurrying over from supervising the table setting. "A bunch of guys are outside with loaded trucks. They all say you asked them to come. What are you doing with my Hall?"

Tyler slapped the man's back. "Feeding people and creating the wedding you had on your agenda. Thank you. You're a good man, Reg." He pointed overhead towards the front doors. "Let's go, guys!"

Reg mouthed words; clearly torn between his slipping control and the compliment. He harrumphed and marched off, issuing orders for the spreading of sand and salt over the parking lot.

Melody took the pen and paper back, whispering to Adelaide. "Go. I've got this."

Adelaide grinned at Melody, then stuffed her arms into her coat sleeves and hustled after Tyler. Outside, there was, indeed, a dozen or so pickups loaded with barbecues of all shapes and sizes. Men of all ages hopped down from the truck cabs and surrounded Tyler. After greetings and guffaws, the group fell silent, listening to the man at their centre.

The man with a plan.

After receiving orders, the new arrivals returned to their trucks, shouldered shovels, and followed Tyler through the foyer of the Hall and out the back. In a crazy short time, they had dumped the deep blanket of snow on the expansive deck over the railing.

Children stormed the cleared space. Their shouts and squeals rang in the clear cold air and echoed over the frozen bay. A heavy sheet of cardboard became an improvised toboggan and other kids flung themselves down the snowbanks created by the shovelling.

By late afternoon, in the Hall's massive kitchen, a crazy quilt assortment of containers lined the back wall and jammed the walk-in cooler and freezer.

Tyler stepped into the middle of his impromptu crew and considered the eager smiling faces around him. "Hi, everyone. Thanks to those of you who emptied out your pantries and freezers. We've got a lot of people to feed with no clue how many or for how long. It's going to be one heck of a potluck. So we'll need to be extremely organized. And on Saturday, we've got LeeAnn and Jesper's wedding, to which you are all invited at Jesper's request. By the way, the wedding is a secret. LeeAnn thinks it's been postponed again, but we have other plans."

One Day Before the Wedding

The next day flashed by in vignettes. Hayley taking a gorgeous *clafoutis* from the oven. A crying toddler slamming into his mother, making her drop her cake. Glory grimacing at the spice combination of a stew. An older woman showing a teen how to knead bread. Tyler walking the barbeque line outside, nudging skill levels a little higher, praising Reg for his incredible ribs. Adelaide showing a small group how to make chocolate ruffles to adorn a cake. A line of cooks making crêpes.

The volume of talk and laughter deafened Adelaide, and she escaped to the only quiet spot in the place—the ladies' room.

Glory and her daughter were at the basins, washing their hands. "Tyler is something else, isn't he?" Glory leaned against the counter after the little girl ran out.

"Yes, he is." Adelaide ducked into a stall, hoping to avoid the inquisition she sensed was coming.

No such luck.

Glory was still there when Adelaide came out. "How long are you in town?"

"Long enough to gas up when the power comes on."

"You coming back?"

Adelaide opened her mouth to say no, but the word stuck in her chest, lodging somewhere near her heart. A bead of sweat trickled down her forehead. She swiped it away with an impatient hand.

"That's what I thought." Glory nodded, uncrossed her arms, and straightened. She paused in the middle of opening the door. "Hurt him and you'll answer to the town."

Adelaide stared at the door long after it had closed behind the other woman. She glanced in the mirror, shocked at the woman who stared back. Who was that messy-haired, rumpled person? Where was the usual perfectly groomed, totally in control woman that Dad expected? The woman in the mirror propped her hands on her hips. "Darned if I know and darned if I care."

Adelaide sank down onto the cushioned bench in the foyer with a grateful sigh. She slipped her shoes off her tired feet, wiggled her toes, and stretched her arches. The kitchen work was thankfully done for the day. Kids slept on cots in the auditorium while groups of adults and teens chatted and laughed in quiet tones. A child fretted in his father's arms; he soothed his son with a snuggle and a kiss.

A mug of coffee appeared in front of her nose. She smiled her thanks and shuffled her butt to one side of the bench.

Tyler slouched beside her with a soft groan. The bruise on his forehead was now a deep ugly purple. "What a day."

She gently kissed his forehead.

He closed his eyes and hummed in appreciation. "Feels better already."

"My poor sweet man. How's your knee?"

He gave her a saucy wink. "In need of a kiss, too."

She giggled at him and changed the topic. "This town is amazing."

He smiled crookedly in acceptance. "Most of the time." He sipped his coffee. "Tell me why you aren't the pastry chef at your family restaurant."

"Umm…." She glanced at the reflection of the people in the dark windows. "I'm not sure I want to spill my guts with your whole town eavesdropping."

He scoffed under his breath. "Standard stuff. You're a new face in a boring situation. Of course, they're watching you."

"Us. They're watching us."

He grinned. "We do tend to look out for our own. It's meant kindly."

She hesitated, sipped her coffee, then pulled a face. "This instant whitener stuff is awful. Why didn't you put out the creamers you brought with us?"

"I'm saving them for the wedding." He rested his hand on top of hers. His caring flowed through her, comforting her. "We've been together a whole three days. I told you my deepest, darkest secret. I sense you have one, too."

She turned her hand over. His palm settled into hers, warm and reassuring. And oh, so sexy. She ran her thumb along his wrist. His pulse quickened, taking hers along on the race. Images of their nights together heated her body as she gazed into his beautiful grey eyes.

"Mommy!" A wide-awake toddler zoomed by.

They both jerked upright, blushing and grinning.

"You were saying…?" he encouraged her.

"I wasn't." She raised a hand to stop his protest. "Okay, okay, short story shorter. Baking is my passion; it's what I'm trained for. Give me flour, butter, sugar—heaven! Meat and veg—no thanks. I had hoped, expected, my uncle would retire, and I'd step into the pâtissier position at The Stone House." She clenched the coffee mug until her fingers hurt. "Dad doesn't dare risk The Reputation on an unproven pâtissier. The front of house is where me and my pretty face belongs, to charm and tempt the clientele into ordering lots of food and wine." She gulped down the rest of the coffee; her mouth puckered at the horribleness. "You know what really grates my nutmeg?"

A smile tugged at his mouth and vanished.

She gave his shoulder a soft nudge with her own. "I've made dozens of wedding cakes and pastries and breads and desserts for family and friends… all with high praises from Dad. But I'm not good enough for his…" swear words clanked in her mind, "…*precious* kitchen."

"Have you ever thought of going out on your own?"

She blinked at his suggestion. "You mean open my own restaurant? In competition with my family?" She hunched her shoulders. """

"The more important question is, could you do it?"

"Darned if I know. Dad would go ballistic. Darned if I care."

Exhausted to his bones, Tyler stretched out on the cot allotted to him for night four of being with Adelaide. Metal frames clanged together as she shoved her temporary bed up against his, as she'd done the previous night. And it surprised her locals showed interest? She's lucky Melody hadn't featured them in a headline: *"Things Heat Up in the Festival Hall Kitchen, Despite Frigid Temps!"* The cot creaked as Adelaide settled in for the night, slipping her hand across his chest to rest over his heart. He laid his own hand over hers, her touch warming him, making him yearn for her tenderness in his life. In a few days, she would leave for her home in Toronto. Would he ever see her again? Did she want to see him?

"LeeAnn is a special woman," she murmured.

He lifted his head in surprise. "Why do you say that?" he whispered back. "Other than what she's done for me, you know nothing about her. Heck, you've never even met her."

"I chatted to a lot of people today. Correction, a lot of people chatted to me. After the weather, she's the number one topic of conversation. Everyone has a story to tell about how she did something for them. Mostly little things. Many with big repercussions. This town loves that woman. Big time."

He lay silent a long time, absorbing this outsider's view of his town. "You're right. LeeAnn is an extraordinary person. Are you jealous?"

"Only if I find out she's gorgeous into the bargain." Her quiet chuckle softened her words.

His own chuckle faded into anxiety. He swallowed hard, clearing his throat. *Suck it up, doofus.* "Um, Adelaide? Um. Will you be coming back to me?"

Her hand clenched his shirt. "Do you want me to come back?"

He lifted her soft hand to his mouth for a kiss. "Yes, I do. So much. Will you come back to me?"

"Yes, I will. Because believe it or not, I love you." She smiled uncertainly into his eyes.

"I believe because I love you back."

With her uncertainty vanished, she huffed a quiet laugh. "If this storm keeps up, I may never actually leave."

"Here's hoping.

THE WEDDING DAY IS HERE

"Tyler. Tyler."

The repeated calling of his name was accompanied by some vigorous pushing against his shoulder. He grumbled and rolled over, smacking into a hard surface with his entire body. The pain, especially in his knee, was horrible. All he could do was groan. He pried his eyes open.

"Poor baby." Soft dark eyes with a hint of laughter met his.

"Adelaide." His loopy smile was unstoppable, as warmth started in his heart and spread through his body.

"So glad you remembered," she teased. "Have you also remembered we have the ultimate winter wedding barbeque feast to finish?"

All the arrangements he'd made yesterday slammed into his mind. With a supreme effort he pushed back onto his knees and sat up.

People around them burst into a cheer. Tyler stumbled on his weak knee as he rose to his feet and bowed to the crowd.

"All right then. Let's get cooking."

DRIFTS OF LACE

Stormy Wedding 4

FOUR DAYS BEFORE THE WEDDING

Chloe Daniels snuggled against her husband Seth. He pulled her closer, into the deep cushions of the brown leather couch, and tucked the granny-square afghan over her shoulders. The Christmas tree twinkled in the corner, surrounded by gifts for Baby.

"What's the weather forecast for tomorrow, my love?" she asked.

Her husband's deep sigh lifted her head. "Didn't you check your own phone?" he asked.

"No, I keep forgetting and the battery's dead. Must be baby brain."

"You gotta stop forgetting. What if you needed help or something?"

"You'd take care of it for me."

"Yes, I would... if I was here."

"And you are here, nice and warm beside me."

With another hard sigh, Seth lifted his phone from the side table, swiped it on, and tapped the weather app. "Not too crazy cold, around freezing. Might turn into freezing rain. A polar vortex is spinning over Manitoba and headed our way. Things could get messy."

She shivered just thinking about it. "Good thing you're not on call. You'll be here to help me if the baby comes a bit early."

He hummed and lifted a thick strand of her straight dark hair to curl around his fingers. "Yeah, we'll cuddle up all weekend long, cozy and warm."

"And safe." She turned to rap on the side table, adding, "Knock on wood."

Seth worked the power lines, a dangerous job. Most of the time, Chloe was okay with the risk. Seth wasn't a dumb guy; he had his electrician's card and had the training for the high-voltage wires. But pregnancy had turned her worry to anxiety. She was terrified of being left pregnant and alone in a small Ontario town more than fifteen hundred kilometers from her family in New Brunswick.

He sighed. "C'mon, honey, we've talked about this. There's nothing to be afraid of."

She pressed against his side, struggling to shift her very pregnant belly and sit upright. The afghan dropped, and cool air slid down her back. She glared at him, frustrated at his continued dismissal of her concerns. "Tell that to Jack's wife and kids the next time they visit his grave."

Seth rubbed a hand down his face. "Jack was cocky—he thought he was untouchable. He didn't respect the danger and paid the ultimate price. You know I never goof around. I take every precaution and then some."

Yes, she knew her terror was irrational, yet nothing anyone said stopped her anxious visions of their fatherless child.

"Did you send in your application to Huron Power?"

He gave a one-shouldered shrug. That meant not yet. "I like my job and I don't want to leave my family. Mom and Dad can't wait to be grandparents for the first time. Besides, there aren't any jobs posted on their website."

It was an endless loop of discussion without resolution; move across the province for a safer indoor job with better pay at the nuclear power plant or stay near his family and risk his life every day.

An uneasy silence filled the room in their red brick house in the heart of Clarence Bay. The flames in the stone fireplace had died down to embers and the chill of the winter night crept in from the edges of the room.

Seth cupped her face. "Please, honey, can we leave the discussion for now? At least until after our baby has met his grandparents?"

She met his concerned gaze. Pale crinkles from squinting in sun, snow, and rain fanned from the corners of his eyes.

"Please, honey?"

She never could resist those big brown eyes. And she did care for his parents and wanted to make them happy. "You know I'm just so worried."

He stroked her forehead to smooth her frown lines. "I love you. Don't worry so much, sweetheart," he murmured as he tipped his head to kiss her, his mouth soft and persuasive, his hug strong and safe.

"I love you back." Chloe pulled his collar aside to nuzzle the curve of his neck and shoulder. He purred when she rose on her knees and tugged his earlobe. She grinned to herself; it worked every time.

A sudden kick from their baby startled them both. Chloe and Seth put their hands on her belly and shared a tender smile at the marvel of new life. Slowly, Baby settled and went back to sleep. Chloe took that as her own cue for bed. She had a busy day ahead with the final adjustments and pressing of LeeAnn's dress. The wedding was four days away.

Yawning hugely, she climbed the stairs to the second storey while Seth extinguished the fire and turned off the downstairs lights. Chloe paused at her workroom door. Bridal gowns shrouded in muslin covers hung like ghosts from the tall rack on one side of her spacious room. Light from the streetlamp struck a gleam off the presser foot of her industrial sewing machine.

Poor LeeAnn, stuffed into a poufy princess dress that overwhelmed her smaller figure. Momzilla insisted that LeeAnn's deceased father had always wanted to walk her down the aisle in such a dress. LeeAnn needed so desperately to prevent her mother's slide back into the depression caused by her father's sudden death three years ago that she'd surrendered all decisions to her mother.

Yes, Chloe knew she sounded like a heartless shrew. But she had enough experience in her dress-making business to recognize emotional blackmail when it bit a bride in the butt.

"So you're almost done with LeeAnn's dress. Isn't she leaving it kinda late, what with the wedding on Saturday?" Seth came behind her and placed his hand on her hip to nudge her towards the bedroom.

"It's not much. A quick zip around the hem on my sewing machine to shorten the skirt by a couple of centimeters."

Seth's eyebrows rose. "A couple of centimeters?" Chloe had told him stories about last-minute changes, but he still found the degree of fussing hard to believe.

"Yep. It can make the difference between a graceful entrance or a disastrous faceplant in the aisle."

"Who knew?" A grin quirked his mouth. "Well, you knew, so that's what counts."

Her wonderful man bent to remove her shoes and help her out of her maternity jeans that she wore with one of his flannel shirts. She cradled his whiskery face as he rewarded himself with kisses on her breasts. It was a while before she got into her tent of a fuzzy nightgown. Loved up and tucked in, Chloe snuggled into Seth's sleepy heat.

Insistent ringing ripped through the depths of treasured sleep. Chloe groaned and shoved at Seth's shoulder. At this time of night, there was only one reason the phone rang—Seth was being called out to work.

Seth mumbled and rolled over.

And the phone kept ringing.

"Seth, answer the phone." She shoved him again.

He grumbled and buried his head under his pillow.

And the phone kept ringing. How could he sleep through it?

"Damn it, Seth." Chloe heaved herself over her lump of a husband, snatched up his phone, and flumped back onto her pillow. "Seth's phone," she barked.

Silence greeted her. "Uh… hi, Chloe. Is uh… is Seth there?" said the gruff voice of Seth's boss, Larry.

"Yeah. Sleeping like the dead man he's gonna be if he doesn't wake up."

Larry laughed.

"Hold on a sec." Chloe put down the phone and reached to turn on the bedside lamp. Nothing happened. No beam of cheerful light pushed back the shadows of the night. There must be a power outage. Well, duh. That's why her lineman husband was getting a call at—no o'clock—the alarm was dark, too.

She hefted her belly over to reach out and tweak the ear she'd nibbled earlier.

"Ouch!" Seth batted her hand away.

"Seth, wake up."

"No."

She tweaked his ear again. "Larry's on your phone."

He groaned, then finally took his phone from her, and slapped it against his ear. "Yeah?" he growled. "It is? For how long? Damn. How widespread do you say? Damn. That's a lot of territory. Yeah. Okay. Overtime is good. Be there as soon as I can."

On her side of the bed, Chloe's heart sank. She knew what came next.

Seth stumbled out of bed and over to the closet. "I gotta go, sweetheart."

"Wasn't Ken supposed to be on call tonight?"

"His wife and kids are sick."

"She's got a mother living near her. Why can't she go over? You just got off shift."

"Her mother's in Florida."

"*Humph.*" She surrendered the argument even though her terror was flaring.

After dressing in layers of warm clothes, he returned to the bed, placed his hands on either side of her shoulders, and leaned down for a kiss.

"Please don't go." She threw her arms around his neck. "We hate being alone at night."

He rubbed her belly. "That's playing dirty, sweetheart. I doubt I'll be out long. The whole town is down, so the break is probably on the main line, and it'll be easy to find."

"I have a real bad feeling about your going."

"You've had bad feelings before, and nothing's come of them."

"But I'm so afraid you'll get hurt."

"It's not like I'm a cop or fireman. Those are dangerous jobs."

"Cops and firemen aren't messing about with 30,000 volts of electricity in a single wire. I don't want you fried to a crisp."

"I won't be fried, nor will I be shot at or have to run into a burning building. You know I'm careful." He gave her a quick kiss and released himself from her grip. "Don't be afraid, sweetheart, I'll be fine. Okay?"

"I hate the thought of being alone."

"If you get frightened, our neighbours will help."

She hung her head. "You're right. I'm sorry to be such a scaredy cat."

He stroked her bent head. "I get it, honey. Your family is across the country, my family is an hours' drive away. But Emma and Meg are just next door, and the midwife is only the other side of town."

She lifted her head, struggling to show a confident smile. "You're right again. Emma and Asher went to St. Lucia. But

Meg is an expert at giving birth. Did you know she's pregnant again? Number five."

"There you go, real help is just a shout away," he said, nudging up her chin with a gentle hand.

She reached out to fix his misbuttoned shirt, then ran her hands down his chest. "You'd better get going. People are depending on you to keep the power running."

"I'll see you later, princess." He blew a kiss from the doorway.

The sounds of Seth donning his heavy outerwear and stomping into his boots was followed by the slam of the door. The gunning of his truck engine vibrated in the room. Silence.

She flopped back onto the rumpled sheets, longing for the safety of her parents' home where they and her four older brothers would take care of their Princess. Her thoughts screeched to a halt. Maybe Seth had a point when he sometimes spoke her family's nickname with a bit of not nice in it. Huh. Had her hovering family, thinking they were being kind, really taught her to be helpless? She grudgingly admitted to herself that she was kinda helpless at times and relied too much on others to fix things. Nudged by her thoughts and Seth's earlier words, Chloe got her phone out of her purse, and put it on the charger.

Baby stirred, pressing on her bladder. As quickly as an almost nine-months-pregnant woman could move, she hustled to the washroom. On the way back to bed, she paused at the window to gaze at the surreal landscape.

Moonlight picked out the ragged edges of clouds in a cold silvery glow. The wind-scraped surface of the bay reflected the shifting light while the town lay dark and nearly invisible below. Traffic radiated out from a spot that might be the Compass, Clarence Bay's favourite place for beer, burgers, and bands. A lone car left the gas station at the edge of town, turned onto James Street, and stopped.

Chloe sighed.

The power outage had given her a unique view of her small town and taken away her husband in the same blink of an eye.

THREE DAYS BEFORE THE WEDDING

Chloe woke to bright sunlight laid in squares across the far wall and pouring over the bed. She dragged the covers tight around her chilled neck and shoulders. As she began to thaw, her cell phone chimed with a text message from Seth, startling her. Snatching the phone off the bedside table, she ran to the wash-room. No one waits for baby bladder.

Still at work. Back at end of shift.

Still here. Love you. xxxx

That's good. Love you, too. xxxx

Making up by text wasn't as much fun as doing it face-to-face, but she'd take what she could get. Chloe cleaned up in rea-sonably warm water. Downstairs in the kitchen, she flipped the switch on the coffeemaker. Darn it. Decaf or not, she needed her coffee. Seth always made the coffee, and having to do it her-self made her miss him more than ever. And how, exactly, was she supposed to make coffee without power?

"There must be more than one way to brew a pot." Her gaze fell on the barbeque out on the deck. Seth always shovelled a path between the door and the barbeque because he grilled year round. "If he can make that thing go, so can I. I'll show him I am not *that* helpless."

No toaster. She'd simply have to make do with bacon and eggs for breakfast. Pity. She grinned.

"Now, what does my grill-freak hubby use to fry on the barbeque?" She poked around in the cupboards and loaded food and equipment on a tray. Then she stuffed her feet into warm boots and tried to close her parka over her belly.

Out on the deck, she turned the centre knob on the barbeque. Where was the flame? Seth always got a pretty blue flame. Arms akimbo, she stared at the metal monster. How did he do it? He pressed a clicky button. After several tries, she found the clicky button, but still no flame. Grrrrr! Maybe if she stared at it hard enough, the thing would burst into flame all by itself. Darn it. Wait, were there words on the front? Instructions! Thank God. *Turn on the gas. Press the clicker.* Poof, a flame. HA! Food, cooking.

After breakfast, she boiled water on the nifty side burner to handwash the dishes. Best to save whatever hot water remained in the insulated tank in the basement. As she climbed the stairs to her workroom, a contraction hit. She breathed through the Braxton Hicks and moments later, she was on her way again, rubbing her belly.

"That was excellent practice, Baby. But it's not quite time for you to come. You stay where it's nice and warm until your daddy gets the lights turned back on."

A gust of wind rattled the old windows in their loose frames. Chloe took a bit of cardboard from a package of seam tape and jammed it into the crack, stopping the noise. The bright sun heated the room. Baby pressed a heel into her bottom rib on the right side.

"Time to play?" Chloe pushed back on the tiny heel with her thumb and waited. As always, Baby pushed back from the inside.

Chloe laughed with pure joy and responded to Baby's kicks several more times. Baby got tired, gave a mighty stretch that forced Chloe to sit up very straight, and settled for a morning nap.

"I hope you sleep as well after you're born." She gave a long rub to the place where the baby's back lay and turned her attention to the work waiting for her. She spread LeeAnn's dress over the table, painstakingly measured and trimmed off the extra centimeters from all the layers, straightening often to ease the cramps in her lower back. Finally, she stepped away from the sewing table.

She shivered. The sun had moved across the sky, taking warmth and light with it.

Baby was practicing yoga again. Or maybe it was Pilates this time. "You're getting very good at that, my little munchkin." She soothed the ache with a firm rub.

She sat down in front of her machine and flipped the switch. The light over the machine's needle didn't come on. Duh. Of course not. No power. "Well then, I'll just do it by hand."

How did one stitch a rolled hem without a machine and the spiffy little presser foot made for doing that and nothing else? Chloe scanned her bookshelf crammed with how-to-sew books, including antique and vintage editions. The *Vogue's New Book for Better Sewing* printed in 1952 had the best answer for silk chiffon.

Chloe practiced on some scraps until she mastered the art of tiny, near-invisible stitches. Lost in the repetitive flash and dance of the fine needle, Chloe barely noticed the time passing. By the time her finicky self was happy, the sun had sunk too low to provide adequate light for handwork. "We'll just have to finish tomorrow. I hate working this close to the deadline, but as long as you stay put, sweet Baby, we'll be fine." She hung the dress on the dummy then gathered the required supplies in one of the many small baskets she used to organize her work. With luck, the power would be back on when she was ready to stitch.

Back downstairs in the living room, she gazed at the cold empty fireplace. Must have heat. How did Seth start a fire?

Sheesh! This was turning into a day of What Would Seth Do? Well, there was wood, newspaper, and matches. How hard could it be? She tossed a few sheets of paper onto the grate, added some chunks of wood, and lit the paper. The paper flared, flames licked at the wood, and went out.

"What the hell?" Chloe sat on the footstool and studied the burnt flakes of paper, then shifted her gaze to the pile of wood. She took the logs out of the grate, re-laid some newspaper, remembering to scrunch it up just like Seth did—sigh—added some small bits of wood, and put back the larger bits of wood. This time the fire caught the skinny pieces of wood which obligingly transferred the fire to the bigger pieces. "HA! Fire, burning."

What to do with herself now? It was too dark to work, the TV needed power, and her ereader had died yesterday. She glanced at her bookshelves. Re-read Georgette Heyer? The author's detailed descriptions of Regency-era clothing had sparked Chloe's interest in gown design. She shivered again. Now she sympathized with the characters' cold dark houses.

Okay, reading it was. But first she needed light. She scrounged around the house, but the only thing she found was the decorative kerosene lamp they'd gotten for a wedding gift and never used. Apparently, the height of the wick was the tricky bit. Too high and it smoked, too low and it went out, just right and it gave a surprising amount of light.

"Lights lit. I am on a roll."

She snuggled under the afghan on the couch. A wood fire and lamplight—the perfect Regency setting.

"Join the chilly club," she muttered. Baby kicked in agreement with her. Chloe straightened to give her child a bit more room. A contraction hit and eased.

"You're getting to be a champion at that, Baby. Just remember, you can't come until Daddy's home."

At the end of his overtime shift at nine o'clock that night, Seth cautiously opened the kitchen door and stepped inside. Triple time was nice and all, and the money would come in handy for all the things the new baby would need, but seventeen hours was more than he'd signed on for. They should hail him as a hero, he grumbled, knowing he'd catch hell from his union rep next week for too many consecutive hours worked. Tired to the bone, he hung up his coat and toed off his heavy boots, then paused and listened. The house was eerily silent. There was no cheery hello, no warm hug, no hot kiss either. Head and shoulders sagging, he crept up the stairs, peeling off his fleece jacket, his flannel shirt and, finally, his t-shirt. He paused at her sewing room and peeked in, just in case. No Chloe there, either.

In the bedroom, he found his wife slumped across the bed, sound asleep, a book askew in her lap, shadows darkening the delicate skin beneath her eyes. His heart squeezed in sympathy. He roused her just enough to help her shift to a more comfortable position, before pulling the blankets over her shoulders and kissing her softly on her cheek.

A wave of exhaustion drove him to take a super quick, chilly shower before crawling into bed and conking out, comforted by the heat of his beloved wife and child.

Two Days Before the Wedding

What felt like seconds later, Seth sat bolt upright in bed. The smell of burning wood had him jumping out of bed and rushing downstairs. His heart slamming against his ribs, he charged into the living room where the sounds and smells were strongest. He skidded to a halt in the arched entryway. Chloe squatted in front of the fireplace, finely balanced between her butt and her belly. It looked really awkward and incredibly sexy at the same time. He groaned under his breath.

Chloe turned at the sound and rose awkwardly, using the mantle for balance. Her welcoming smile warmed him all the way down to the chilled soles of his feet.

"Good morning!" She came to him, belly first, arms wide.

He pulled her to him, leaning forward from his hips to kiss her soundly.

His wife's eyes fluttered open with the sleepy sexy look that always turned him on. Her gaze sharpened as she read the expression on his face. "What's wrong?"

He stroked her arms to keep them around him. "I have to go out again."

She stepped back, out of his arms, worry creasing her brow.

He clasped her hands, hoping to ease her fear. "All leave has been cancelled. Everybody who's in the country has to show up. Guys from other provinces are coming to help."

Baby moved beneath her stretched-tight t-shirt. Instead of the usual beach ball shape, it was more like she'd swallowed a giant football. She drew a deep breath, exhaling on a slow count as she caressed their child. "It's okay, Baby. Daddy will be home as soon as he can. I don't like it any better than you do, but that's life when your daddy's a lineman. Now, you stay put until he's back home to catch you."

Her soothing voice settled all three sets of nerves.

"I'm sorry I'm such a grouch. My worries are getting to me. I'll manage." She sighed deep and long. "The outage is really serious, then?"

"The whole of Toronto and all the way up to north of Clarence Bay district. If the outage goes on much longer, I want you to go to my parents in Sudbury. I called, and Dad will drive down and pick you up."

She shuddered visibly at the suggestion of a long tense drive on a winter highway, then squared her shoulders. "Go and get dressed. Your breakfast is waiting for you under warm dishtowels."

Relieved at her acquiescence, he teased her with a sceptical look.

She crossed her arms and waggled her head in light-hearted smugness. "Yes, it really is there despite the power outage. I'm not such a princess after all." She giggled sheepishly. "Umm… would you push the couch closer to the fire for me, so we'll be warmer?"

After a shared chuckle, a couple of shoves saw the job done. When he went in for a delicious kiss from his wife, Baby kicked against his lower abdomen. He played a brief game of kick-and-poke with his unborn child, grinning like a fool the whole time. Chloe's giggles kept time. When the little one tired, Seth went back upstairs to get dressed.

Once bundled up and ready to go, Seth went to the living room to say goodbye to Chloe. She sat on the brown leather couch, with LeeAnn's wedding dress spread over her lap, plying her needle in the delicate fabric. Seth placed a hand on the back of the couch and bent to kiss her upturned face. He straightened and glanced at the low-burning fire and the almost gone wood-pile. "I'll bring in some more wood before I go."

"Thanks, love. You look after us so well." She gave her big tummy a little pat. She folded the dress over the arm of the couch and reached out her hands. "Before you go out, would you help me up? I need to use the washroom."

He grasped her hands and pulled her to her feet. Quick as she could, she was out of the room and down the hall.

Smiling at her brisk waddle, Seth continued on his way through the kitchen to the mudroom where he hauled on boots and jacket. Outside, he shovelled through the new-fallen snow to the bare earth and sawdust of the path around the corner of the house. Arms loaded with firewood; he elbowed his way back through the mudroom door.

A loud scream tore through the silent house.

"Chloe!" Seth dropped the logs and clomped into the living room as fast as his big snowy boots allowed. Chloe stood in front of the open fire, the screen to one side, the last log at her feet. Hands clamped over her mouth did nothing to mute her continued shrieking. Her wide eyes focussed on the dress.

The dress was on fire!

Seth clomped over and stomped on the dress, snuffing the fire, then clasped Chloe by the shoulders. "Are you okay?"

Hands still over her mouth, her huge, rounded eyes stared at him.

"Chloe, are you burned anywhere?"

Slowly, she shook her head.

He lay a gentle hand on her tummy. "Is the baby okay?"

Slowly, she nodded.

"Then what's wrong?"

As if in a trance, Chloe pointed at the dress.

He glanced over his shoulder, then turned fully. "Fuck," he whispered.

The layers of fabric had melted back from the now-dead ember that had snapped out of the fire. One great big, dirty, sawdusty boot print decorated the skirt of the pristine wedding gown.

He stared at it, dumbfounded, his jaw working to find words that would match the horror. "I'm... Fuck!... so, so, so sorry."

"It... it's not your fault. You p-put out the fire. You s-saved m-me." She clamped a hand over her trembling mouth. Tears welled in her eyes.

Another ember snapped out of the fire, landing safely on the tile hearth. Chloe jolted. Seth put the dropped log on the fire and replaced the screen.

"Oh, Seth." Her voice warbled as she leaned into him, turning away from the destruction. He wrapped his arms around his upset wife, cupping the back of her head to offer what little comfort he could.

"Is it fixable, sweetheart?"

She lifted her head from his shoulder. "I need more fabric. But I can't get it. I need to use my sewing machine. But I can't turn it on." Her voice caught, and she swallowed painfully. "I need more time to rebuild the dress by hand. But I don't have it. The wedding's in two days."

"So, no?"

Tears rolled down her cheeks. "N-no."

Her phone shattered the shocked silence.

She glanced at the screen. "Oh, my God. It's Jesper." Panic stalled her tears. She put it on speaker. "Jesper, what's wrong? Is everything okay? LeeAnn? Her mom? Tell me it's not her mom."

"Sorry to scare you. We're all good," Jesper said, his voice tight and whispery.

Chloe sagged against Seth, limp with the relief that hit him just as hard. They held each other up.

"I'm running out of battery, so I gotta talk fast."

"Go."

"Will you shorten LeeAnn's dress the way she first wanted it?"

Chloe blinked. "I thought LeeAnn had decided—"

"No, she didn't. She caved to her mother. Can you make it right?"

"Uh… sure."

"Norah wants to cancel the wedding again and LeeAnn's really upset and crying."

Chloe gasped, then gestured wildly at Seth to hand her the dress. He passed it to her, and she held it up against him. Of course, he was taller than LeeAnn, but Chloe's experienced eye made design adjustments and calculations. All the damage was at the bottom—the part Jesper had just asked her to cut off. "Thank goodness," she breathed.

"Uh, Chloe? Repeat, please. I missed that," Jesper's voice called from her hastily dropped phone.

"Just a practice contraction," she fibbed. "I'll shorten the dress, no problem. Consider it done."

"Same time and day as scheduled at the Festival Hall, Saturday, four PM."

"Sure. Why?" Chloe waiting for a response. When none came, she said, "Jesper? Jesper? Are you still there?"

Jesper was gone, his battery obviously dead.

"Everything okay?" Seth asked.

"Yeah. He warned me his phone was nearly out of juice right up front." She swiped off her phone and grinned at Seth and wiped her eyes.

"So you can fix it?"

"Yep. The Christmas Spirit was listening, because now I can give my best friend in the world the wedding dress of her dreams."

Best friends in the world didn't even begin to describe the relationship. Chloe and LeeAnn had fallen into sisterhood at first sight in junior kindergarten. They'd supported each other through grade school, high school, and by phone and videos while attending separate colleges. Once they'd both returned to Clarence Bay, LeeAnn had promoted the heck out of Chloe's new business; first by setting up a custom dressmaking website, then ensuring that Melody Grisham regularly featured the up-and-coming designer Chloe Daniels in the Hatch, Match, and Dispatch column in the *Clarence Bay Beacon*. In the two years since opening her doors, eighteen brides had ordered gowns for themselves and their parties. All thanks to LeeAnn.

"That's awesome, sweetheart, Seth said. "I know you'd do anything for LeeAnn. And so would I. But… I gotta go." He hesitated, fearing his wife's response.

Chloe drew a breath… and stopped. "Yes, you do. I'll see you when you get home. Baby and I will be busy sewing."

Chloe smiled to herself as she folded and pinned the dress so the hideous boot print didn't spread it's dirt and sawdust, then carried it upstairs to her sewing room.

Seth had been shocked and relieved when she casually saw him on his way. Shamefaced, she realized what a burden she must have been. Well, no more.

As she leaned over to spread the skirt across her worktable, a twinge shot through her lower back. It passed in moments. Hmm. From her file cabinet, she pulled out the design folder and reviewed all the decisions and measurements. Yes, there it was, the original below-the-knee design and its full-length rendition.

The worst part of being a wedding dress designer was bearing silent witness to raging battles between brides and mothers, with family and friends aligned on both sides. LeeAnn and Norah both had strong opinions about what the dress should be like—

classic Audrey Hepburn cocktail dress vs Disney princess poufy gown. Clients seldom asked Chloe for her opinion, though she always had one. In LeeAnn's case, she'd agreed with the bride. A shorter dress suited LeeAnn's figure and personality.

LeeAnn's dress had been in the early design stage three years ago when her father had died of a sudden heart attack, and they'd postponed the wedding. This past summer, LeeAnn's mom had finally shown an interest in The Wedding.

Chloe consulted her trim notes. Here, again, was evidence of a pitched battle. Multiple sketches bore many modifying pencil strokes. Staple holes perforated the heavy paper where fabric and trim samples had been approved then removed.

LeeAnn had won most decisions, using Chloe's expert opinions to support her wins. Normally, Chloe was quite happy to be excluded from these family squabbles, but in this case, she gone to bat for her friend. Two against one should have carried the day, especially since it was LeeAnn's wedding. But Norah had broken out the ultimate weapon—tears. Eventually, Lee-Ann had caved and agreed to the princess pouf. Thank goodness they had at least compromised, agreeing to lose the train and bustle. This made Chloe's adjustments easier to do by hand.

Still, it would take hours.

"It's not like we have anything else to do, eh, little one?"

The little one replied with a kick.

"Ow. That was my kidney. Watch your aim, Baby." She stroked over the baby's back. "How about you practice your soccer kicks after lunch? Maybe Daddy will be back by then."

Chloe measured and trimmed away the excess fabric, restoring the garment's pristine whiteness. The horrible footprint slithered into the waste bin, and the leftover satin would make an elegant memento bag. The lace might make… what? Something to think about while she hemmed.

Ready to start over again, Chloe made her way back to the living room couch where the cushions were softest, and the lighting was best. She reached for the remote to click on the TV for company, chuckling at herself when she remembered the TV—like everything else that ran on electricity—was down for the count. Instead, she hummed softly to herself and her unborn child.

She fell into her rhythm as she sewed her tiny, perfect stitches. Every once in a while, she stopped stitching to refuel the fire, being extra careful to place the dress out of range of spitting embers. Rubbing her eyes and straightening her back, Chloe gave some thoughts of admiration to all the dressmakers throughout history who had created such marvels of ingenuity with only a needle and thread, while working by candlelight. It made her long for the time when the power came back on.

In the hours creeping to sunset, she laid in the final stitch on the much shorter hem. Taking the dress upstairs, she draped LeeAnn's wedding dress on the dressmaker's dummy. The skirt stuck out like a bizarre tutu. Out came the scissors to cut large triangles out of some of the layers of crinoline. Now the skirt had an unusual swingy quality. *Cool. Note to self for future reference.*

She yawned. Tomorrow was another day. Pleased with herself, she went downstairs to cook a can of soup over the fire and sleep fitfully on the couch, wrapped burrito-style in the duvet from the bed. In the middle of the night, she woke to shiver her way to the washroom and back. On the way, she stopped to grab a toque from the closet. She'd never understood why people in the olden days had worn caps to bed. Now she knew.

One Day Before the Wedding

At the crack of dawn the next morning, Seth hauled his exhausted self into the passenger seat of the bucket truck. They'd spent the night in a rundown motel along Highway 400. Chloe had been surprisingly chill with the news. Seth had lost track of how many downed wires they'd repaired as they made their way back through the towns and hamlets of the Medonte Valley.

"Where to today?" he asked Will, his co-worker behind the wheel.

"Clarence Bay district."

"'Bout damn time."

"You worried about Chloe? She's due soon, eh?"

"Any day now. I hope she waits until we get power back, so I can be with her."

"You're going into the delivery room?"

"She wants me there. Can't say I'm keen on watching a baby split my wife in two."

Will shuddered. "I couldn't watch that part either. For any of my kids. Focus on Chloe's face and do whatever she tells you. Rub her back, give her ice, turn the pillow, let her break your hands when she squeezes down, whatever. You'll be so busy, you won't see anything until the doctor lays the munchkin on Mommy's chest."

Seth swallowed hard, a little green around the gills.

Will laughed and punched his shoulder. "Don't worry, pal. If you faint, they shove you to one side and get on with doing their jobs."

"I'm not planning on fainting."

"Yeah. But birthing a baby isn't the same as dealing with a broken arm. It's more—uh… messy and… gross and… cool."

A fine sweat chilled Seth's back despite his heavy clothes.

Driving up the highway in broad daylight, the destruction done by the ice storm was some scary shit. Ice coated everything, trees bowed under the weight. "Don't worry, buddy. You'll do just fine. It's just—"

They had barely crested a hill, when, without warning, a massive tree split down the middle. Half of it crashed to the ground. Shards of ice and broken branches sprayed the area. The other half hit another tree on the way down. In an instant, a swath of trees from hilltop to highway had toppled. The area looked like it had been clear cut by over-enthusiastic lumberjacks.

Will slowed the truck, careful of treacherous black ice, and pulled over to the side of the highway. Both men waited, jaws gaping, breaths held, and fingers crossed that the power lines would escape.

The final tree in the domino line shuddered with the impact of its fallen mates. It tilted downhill towards the power line… and held firm.

The cab steamed as the men exhaled in relief.

Too soon. The tree released its largest branch and laid it, oh so gently, on the power line.

Seth's breath jammed in his throat. Beside him, Will sucked in air.

The line sagged under the wooden weight, stretched way taut. The poles on either side leaned hard towards each other like drunken goal posts.

Shockingly, everything held.

Seth and Will exchanged bug-eyed stares.

"Damn!"

"Crap!"

"That's going to be a bitch to deal with."

"Huge bitch."

Seth called in the situation while Will positioned the truck and lowered the braces to stabilize the vehicle.

The two men stood by the truck and assessed the situation.

"Your turn in the bucket, pal." Will punched Seth on the shoulder.

Seth sighed, clambered in, and harnessed up. The public thought the bucket was a lot of fun. So had Seth, the first time. Until he'd witnessed Jack getting tossed to the ground when he accidentally made contact with the 30,000 volts in a live wire. Power lines didn't come with switches to flip or plugs to pull to turn off the power. All you had to do to avoid electrocution was take tremendous care *not to touch the damn wire!*

The crews were warned repeatedly. *Always assume a wire was live. Never take chances. Focus like your life depends on it.*

Because it did.

Using the controls in the bucket, Seth manoeuvred into place beside the branch. He examined the branch's structure, looking for the best place to hook it and lift. There it was, the perfect V. He threaded a broad strap around the highest notch, making sure to leave enough slack. Feathering the controls, he backed the bucket out.

If he was too slow, the bucket would stall.

Too fast and the wire would rebound, flinging the branch, and itself, against the bucket.

Harness or not, fibreglass bucket or not, there would be absolute hell to pay.

The branch could snap in two where the strap held, fall onto the wire, and set off a rebound.

Or it could snag the wire. Then there'd be a delicate dance with a chainsaw, a branch, and that 30K. It was never a certainty where the debris would fall.

Adrenaline prickled over Seth's shoulders and back. His hand trembled on the controls, jiggling them.

The bucket bounced.

Seth's heart boomed in his ears.

"Easy, buddy." Will's voice came from below, steadying his nerves.

Seth dragged in a breath and released it. Grasping the controls, he started his upward journey.

The branch twirled as the notch lifted from the wire. Seth leaned over the edge to grab it and halt the perilous spin. The harness bit into his shoulders through his jacket and the thick layers beneath.

Seth continued the lift in that position, hanging over the edge, using the controls by instinct. High, high, higher he went, until the tiniest twig on the tip of the branch cleared the wire. Seth swung the bucket away from the danger zone. Checking for ground clearance, he lowered bucket and branch. Finally, close enough to the ground, he released the branch and stowed the bucket.

"Good stuff, Seth buddy. Good stuff." Will slapped Seth on his back. "Now let's get back on the road home and hope nothing else gets in the way."

Seth and Will continued north under darkening skies, scanning the lines for breaks. They found and fixed several more. Electricity followed them, humming along the wires. None of the fixes were as dramatic as the cascade of ice-laden trees in the Medonte Valley, just your average break due to ice on the line.

They stopped for lunch at Sellar's Cove Inn, sputtering on the last of the gas in its generator. The owner was so happy to see them, she'd given them huge hugs and a free lunch. A pack of sandwiches and a Thermos of coffee left the restaurant with them. Who needed a badge or a gun to be a hero?

They reached the town of Clarence Bay by mid-afternoon. Seth texted Chloe again to check on her. Each time, he'd received a cheery reply. This time, however, there was no reply at all.

"Her battery musta died," Will said.

"Logical explanation."

"Still doesn't stop you from worrying."

"Nope."

"We've got our choice of places to start checking the lines, so why don't we start on your street, eh?"

"Thanks, Will."

Will turned onto Louisa Street and slowed to a crawl past Seth's house. A steady stream of smoke rose from his chimney. Chloe was warm, sitting in a chair pulled up to the living room window, reading a book. His soul eased.

Will tooted the horn. She lifted her head, grinned, and waved.

Now Seth could focus on his work. They drove another kilometer to the end of his long twisty street then dipped into a shallow valley. Right away, they found the line on the road beneath a row of shattered trees. It would take hours to clear away the debris before they could even think about the wires.

The smile on Chloe's face faded as she hunched over in the window seat and blew out her breath through a contraction. When it eased less than a minute later, she straightened and ran a calming hand over her tummy. "Was that a practice contraction or a real one?" Just to be on the safe side, she picked up her phone to start the countdown app. Dead. Hold on, Seth bought a portable charger. Where the heck was it? While she racked her brains over the location, another contraction hit, mild, short. Showtime?

Where the fu—? Mustn't swear in front of Baby! Where the blankety-blank was that blankety-blank charger?

She stood, taking several deep breaths to calm her mind. Was the charger in her hospital bag along with a clean nightgown and a change of clothes? She shivered her way through the cold hallway and up into the bedroom. Sure enough, it was in the bag in the closet.

"Thank God for a man who plans," she muttered.

Never again would she accuse her handsome husband of fussing too much. Back downstairs, she plugged in her phone and waited for enough charge to make a call.

She growled in frustration. "Blankety-blank-blank-blank! No signal?!" Even a princess couldn't fix that.

Another contraction hit, stronger and longer than all the others. "Now you choose to arrive, baby? You couldn't have waited just one bitty day more?" She set the timer on her phone to track the spacing of the contractions.

"Okay, Baby, it's you and me. What would Daddy do?" She snorted. "Daddy, schmaddy. What would Trixie of *Call the Midwife* do? They did births in some dire places. What are we gonna do?" She stroked her tummy. "We, my sweetie, are gonna have ourselves a home birth in front of the fire. And pray for some bars on the phone."

Hold on. Meg, mother of four with one on the way, would help her. She hustled to the front window, only to see her neighbour's empty driveway. Where had they gone? Didn't matter now.

Chloe waddled around the house, collecting anything she thought might be of use—tarp, blankets, towels, scissors and thread—she shuddered at that—warm socks, more wood.

A half-hour later, Chloe stood, arms akimbo, assessing her preparations.

"Okay, Baby, I'm ready."

After repairing a complex break, Seth took a moment to check out his house from the high view in the bucket. Was there less smoke from the chimney? The uneasy feeling of earlier in the day settled in his gut. Nah, it was just his viewpoint from several streets over and almost level with the top of the chimney because of the rise in the hill. The smoke thickened, and he relaxed. Chloe had just stoked the fire.

But his uneasiness didn't lessen. As they crept closer to his street, that rising column of smoke waxed and waned. His worry rose and fell along with it.

The final time he was in the bucket, no smoke at all smudged the air, and his worry changed to fear. He lowered the bucket.

"What's up?" Will asked.

"Can you keep going without me? I gotta check on Chloe."

"Can't you just call her?"

"There's no signal, and something feels wrong. I have to go."

Will checked his watch and looked into Seth's eyes. "There's only an hour left in the shift."

Seth's shoulders slumped. "Geez, man, cut me a break, will ya? Chloe's pregnant and cold and alone. She needs me more than you do for the next hour."

Will crossed his arms over his chest. "All right, get lost."

Seth jogged to the truck and opened the door.

"One more thing," Will called.

Seth halted, waiting for the mercurial Will to change his mind.

"I don't want to see your scrawny ass until you're a daddy."

Seth stared at his hard-as-nails partner.

Will's scowl deepened. "You got thirty seconds to get gone, or it's back to work."

Seth grabbed his gear and was gone before Will stopped talking. He ran up the hill and around the corner as fast as he could in all his heavy winter clothes and clunky boots.

On the way, a puff of smoke rose from his chimney. He wanted to slow down, but his anxiety whipped him on. He arrived at his front door gasping and sweating like a horse at the end of the race of the century, shaking so much from the mad dash through deep snow over slick ice that he had to use a double-fisted grip to put the key in the lock.

"Chloe," he called the moment he stumbled through the door. Silence was his only answer. "Chloe, honey, where are you?" No sooner had the sound of his voice faded than a loud grunt drew him to the living room.

A blue plastic tarp showed around the edges of a thick padding of blankets and towels. On her knees, leaning against a kitchen chair, was Chloe, dressed in her oldest housecoat, a flannel nightgown, and a pair of his heavy wool socks. Her hands had a white-knuckled grip on the chair and her back was arched. Her face, half hidden by her hair, was contorted and purple. From between clenched teeth, she uttered a horrific groan that ripped Seth to his very soul.

The sound snapped him out of his stupor. He flung off the outer layer of padded jacket. The laces of his second boot snarled under his hasty fingers. Scrabbling for his pocketknife, he sliced through the lace, threw off padded trousers and boots in one go. He knelt beside his labouring wife and brushed sweaty strands of hair from her face.

"I'm here, honey." He surprised himself with how calm and reassuring he sounded. "We'll get through this."

His words seem to drain the tension from the bow of her back. Her head lowered to the seat of the chair. "Seth." Great sobs racked her.

Seth lifted her arms from her chair and set himself in its place, facing her, both of them on their knees. He wrapped Chloe's arms around his neck.

She jammed her face into the soft flannel of his shirt and sobbed her heart out.

Fear screamed along Seth's nerves. With shaking hands, he cradled her against him. "Shh, honey. It's okay. I'm here. We can do this. Together."

Why did his reassurance only make her cry louder?

Another contraction hit. Her arms tightened around his neck until he thought she was going to break it.

Did he hold strong or bend with her? They hadn't covered this delivery position in pre-natal class. A midwife was supposed to be in charge.

Chloe's long, drawn-out moan filled his ears.

Widening the stance of his knees, he held strong until the contraction passed.

After a few moments of rest, his wife lifted her blotchy, tear-stained, sweaty face.

He swept her sticky hair back and cupped her cheek. "Hi, beautiful." His voice quavered with love.

A weak smile briefly shaped her mouth. She shivered violently.

He drew as close as their baby would allow, running his hands up and down her back until she relaxed against him. Releasing her, he reached for some firewood, only to find the basket empty.

"Will you be okay while I fetch more wood?"

"Yes." She sank onto her knees and slouched over the chair on her forearms. Her sweet face was white with dark shadows under her tired eyes.

He ran like his ass was on fire. Still, he wasn't fast enough. Chloe was mid-contraction by the time he was back. He dropped most of the wood on the floor and threw some in the fireplace. He'd worry about draught and smoke spillage some other time. Kneeling beside his wife hunched over the chair, Seth waited until Chloe relaxed, then settled her on her side on the floor. As he brushed her hair back, his hand touched the collar of her sweat-soaked nightgown. No wonder she was cold.

While rummaging through her dresser for dry clothes, he checked his phone, praying for a signal. Thank you! He called 9-1-1.

"Please state the nature of your emergency."

"My wife's in labour."

"Hi Seth. This is Celina. How far along is Chloe now?"

"You know? And there's no ambulance here yet?" He was shouting but didn't care.

"Chloe called when she had bars for a minute. Isn't the midwife there yet?"

"We're not supposed to have the baby at home! Where is the god-damn ambulance?!"

"Attending a multi-car pileup on the highway. The police took all the paramedics, even the off-duty ones. All the docs are here, waiting."

The meaning of that finally got through Seth's anger. "Shit."

"Yeah. So… the midwife hasn't arrived. Did Chloe call her?"

"Don't know."

"How far along is Chloe?" Celina asked again.

"Uh…" Seth grabbed up the nightgowns he'd found and hustled back to the living room to ask. Chloe groaned an answer he couldn't make out. "Dunno and Chloe can't talk right now."

"Okay. Let me connect you to your midwife. Annalise, right?" A series of clicks sounded, and a super cheery voice rang in his ear.

"Can you tell me how dilated she is?" Annalise asked.

Seth gulped, swallowing hard. He'd done the required reading, watched the films the birthing coach had shown, so he knew what he had to do. Will had said he wouldn't actually have to look. Well, now he'd have to. Carefully. Thoroughly. And report back in detail.

"She, uh, the baby…" He took a deep breath. What he was going through was nothing compared to what Chloe faced. He went over to his wife, kissed her cheek, and bent down to take a look. "Hair. She's, uh, dilated enough that I can see a small circle of hair. I think she's at, maybe, eight or nine centimeters."

Annalise listened and asked more questions. "Things seem to be progressing as they should. Keep her comfortable. Give her sips of water through a straw. I'm on snowshoes thanks to a frozen engine, so I'll get there as soon as I can. Hang tight and leave the front door unlocked. I'm leaving home now. I can't stay on the line but call if you need me." She disconnected.

Seth snarled at the phone. "Damn chirpy woman."

Keep her comfortable. Well, he could do that. Back upstairs, he rummaged some more through drawers and cupboards. He really should do laundry more often, so he'd know where stuff was kept. Just because Chloe worked from home shouldn't mean she had to do all the housework.

Between contractions, Seth cleared away the soaked towels, stripped his wife, and dressed her in warm dry clothes. He couldn't help but grin at her getup of flannel nightgown, two of his flannel shirts, and another pair of his heavy socks. He piled more wood on the fire and was rewarded when Chloe stopped shivering.

Seth tried to convince her to lie down, but she refused. She wanted to kneel and hang on to either him or the chair, preferably him.

Three quarters of an hour later, Chloe climbed to her feet. Leaning on his shoulders, she ordered, "Catch the baby."

Seth cupped his hands between her legs. "Please don't let me drop him. Please don't let me drop him." He didn't realize he was praying aloud until the baby, wet and slippery and screaming his head off, slid into his waiting hands.

With a quiet groan, Chloe plopped her butt on the floor then slumped to her side onto the blankets Seth had piled up for her. The umbilical cord pulsed and stilled.

"It's a boy! I mean, he's a boy!" Bawling to match his son, Seth clamped and cut the cord like the videos had demonstrated. He dried the wee boy and wrapped him in the waiting flannelette sheet and baby blanket Chloe had quilted months ago. She levered herself to a sitting position and he handed the squalling bundle to his mother. The newborn quieted, then opened his eyes to stare myopically at his grinning parents. He hiccupped, and his besotted parents laughed with delight.

"Well done, you two," the midwife called cheerily from the doorway. "Looks like I arrived just in time for cleanup." Annalise leaned over and checked out the newest arrival. "A fine healthy baby boy." She handed the baby to Seth. "Dad, you're on duty now while Mom and I finish up."

Mom and Dad. Chloe and Seth exchanged huge grins at their new names.

A while later, Chloe sat on the couch with baby Adam cradled in her arms. Seth sat with his arm around them both. Before settling in with his new family, Seth had lugged the soiled towels and blankets to the basement to wait for washing.

Annalise zipped her backpack closed and dusted her hands. "Now we just need to move Mom and baby to the hospital."

Alarm crashed through Seth. "Why? What's wrong?"

"Nothing at all. But there's heat and light in the maternity ward."

A resounding knock shook the front door, then Will threw it open and clomped down the hall. "All done, eh? Need a lift?"

Seth grinned at his buddy, then rosed and leaned over to help Chloe stand. "Looks like our ride is here, sweetheart."

THE WEDDING DAY IS HERE

Outside his wife's hospital room, Seth leaned against the wall, deeply happy to have a healthy baby boy, deeply thankful that he'd been there for Chloe in her time of need, and deeply regretful she'd almost done it alone. What if something had gone wrong? What about the future? He shuddered, his stomach clenching with worry.

"Are you okay, Seth?"

He opened his eyes to find Melody Grisham, gossiper extraordinaire, peering at him with concern. "I'm fine, just tired." No way was he saying one word to hang on the town's grapevine.

"I heard yesterday was quite a day for the Daniels's household."

"I guess the grapevine never sleeps," Seth said grumpily. He wasn't a fan of having his business broadcast all over town.

"Nor freezes," Melody replied with a grin, probably used to getting flack for her gossipy role.

"Is that you, Melody?" Chloe called from the hospital room.

A huge smile lit Melody's face. She grabbed Seth's arm and dragged him into the room. "Look who I found lurking in the hall."

Chloe lifted her gaze from their nursing infant. She lifted a beckoning hand to Seth, and he rushed to her side. Chloe raised her face. "Will the new daddy give the new mommy a kiss?"

Seth cupped his wife's cheek in his hand and gazed down into the depths of her shining brown eyes.

"I love you so much, Chloe. I don't know what I would have done if something had happened to you yesterday." He swallowed down his harsh emotions.

Her eyes shone even brighter. "But nothing did happen, so leave it be, and stop worrying so much." She giggled at his surprise. "I worried so much because I felt helpless. After these few days, I know I'm not. I can do things on my own, though I'm so grateful you were there for Adam's arrival. Now, where's my kiss?" She lifted her face a little higher and Seth leaned down for a soft wondrous kiss.

A squawk from their son interrupted them. They chuckled and gazed at the small bundle of squirming humanity in her arms.

Flying on instinct, Seth tucked the child against his shoulder and rubbed the tiny back. The baby let out an immense belch and settled quietly. The three adults snickered at such a thunderous noise from such a wee body.

A nudge from Melody made Seth stand back so she could move around the bed to give her friend a giant bear hug.

"Thanks for coming, Mel. It couldn't have been easy."

Melody settled in the visitor's chair. "It's news, so I'm here. Now tell me all about it."

Chloe laughed and dove into the tale of the snowbound birth. "The whole time I was working on LeeAnn's dress—by hand, by daylight and lamplight—this little fellow was telling me he was ready to—Oh, my God." Chloe threw back the covers and stood wavering, but still meaning to leave.

Melody pushed her back down onto the bed. "You aren't going anywhere, young lady. The dress can wait until the wedding."

"It's today! The wedding is today! This afternoon at the Festival Hall. I told Jesper I'd deliver the entire ensemble: dress, veil, shoes, coat—everything to the Hall for a four o'clock wedding. Today!"

Her husband moved to stand immediately in front of her and laid a hand on her shoulder. "You, my beautiful wife, are not going anywhere."

"But—" Chloe's phone rang, startling the little one.

Seth walked into the hall, jiggling his son back to sleep, gesturing for Melody to follow. The reporter followed grudgingly, without a shred of shame at being caught trying to eavesdrop.

"Hey, Shelby, Chloe said. Thank heavens the hospital had power and signal for her phone. "How's it going?"

"Have you got any fabric you're not using?"

"Why do you want fabric, and how much and what kind?"

"I need enough to make a canopy over a bed so we can turn an office into a wedding suite."

"Sounds lovely... except I'm in hospital."

Shelby gasped. "Are you and the baby okay?"

"Totally fine. Little Adam arrived yesterday."

"Amazing!" Shelby said into the phone before announcing, "Hey, everybody! Chloe had a boy! Adam!"

Chloe laughed as muted cheers and congratulations filled her ear. There was no need for an announcement now. Melody would find herself scooped.

Coming back on the line, Shelby said. "That's wonderful. I'm so happy for you both." "Hold on a sec," Chloe told Shelby. "Melody!" she called out.

Seth and Melody came back into the room.

"Melody, will you go with Seth to our place to pick up the wedding dress and some other stuff and deliver it to the Hall? Shelby has an idea for an office makeover."

"Yeah, sure." A wide grin of anticipation spread across her face. Melody did love to get involved.

"You can take the bolt of red and white jacquard from the bottom rail in my sewing room."

"I think I remember that. A bride insisted on it and then changed her mind, right? It'll be perfect for a Christmas honeymoon suite."

"Yes, that's the one. You'll find embroidery hoops in the cupboard to hang it from. Take some pins, clamps, and fabric tape as well. Oh, and please take some detailed in-progress pictures for me so I can do it again?"

"Photos in progress. Got it." Melody typed the last item into her phone. She leaned in to kiss Chloe's cheek and danced her way out of the room.

"Thanks." Chloe put the phone back to her ear. "Melody will deliver the wedding outfit and some red and white fabric to the Hall."

"Perfect. I'll add some red and white ribbon from the flower shop. And I've got some silk poinsettias and greenery. It'll be gorgeous."

After a few more minutes of chat, Chloe hung up the phone. Seth nestled the baby in Chloe's arms, gave her a kiss, and left them in the quiet of the sunny hospital room. He needed lunch.

Chloe smiled down at her son. "What do you think, young man?"

He blinked up at her and yawned.

"I hear you, sweetie. Time for a nap." As her son drifted off, she smiled to herself. She'd received the best Christmas gift of all.

STORMY WEDDING

Stormy Wedding 5

FOUR DAYS BEFORE THE WEDDING

"Four more sleeps until you're mine." LeeAnn stepped into her fiancé's embrace, unwilling to say goodnight without one more sweet kiss. They stood in the chilly foyer of his family's century-old farmhouse about thirty minutes north of Clarence Bay.

"I can't wait until I'm yours forever and always." Jesper cupped her face in his strong hands and kissed the tip of her nose.

She grinned as he recited a few words from the marriage vows they'd written and practiced. "Forever and always is right," she said ruefully. "I can't tell you how happy I am that you're still here with me, still wanting to marry me."

"I fell in love with you when you smacked me with a snowball in sixth grade. It's impossible to stop now." He wrapped his arms tighter around her. "You're stuck with me."

"Good. Just the way I like it." He gave her a quick kiss. "Think we can fit in another first dance practice?"

She smiled at him. His nervousness about the wedding was adorable. "Of course. I'll come over Thursday night. I hope Mom won't be too upset when we surprise her with our own first dance choice."

"When she sees how graceful you are, she'll get over it."

"For that lovely compliment, you get a kiss." She tucked her hands in his back jeans pockets and pressed against his hard farmer's body. He hummed his appreciation. She tipped her head up for the kiss she wanted more than her next breath.

"Jesper, your mother is a wonderful cook. No one does a roast pork dinner better. And it was such a pleasure to see your brothers again. It's good to see you keeping your Danish heritage active, calling your parents *Mor* and *Far*, and that *gløgg* is a powerful drink."

There went their privacy. Mom had come into the foyer ready to leave. She lifted LeeAnn's mustard-yellow parka from the hook and handed it to Jesper so he could help LeeAnn slide into it. Norah insisted on old-fashioned courtesies. LeeAnn admitted she enjoyed the feeling of being cherished by Jesper.

"The wind has picked up considerably and I want to get home. I still have a number of details to go over before The Wedding which is in only four days." To LeeAnn's ear, Mom always capitalized The Event.

LeeAnn kept her exasperation under wraps, though she couldn't resist sharing a speaking glance with Jesper. "Mom…" She grasped her by the shoulders and looked straight into her eyes. "Stop obsessing. Everything's all set. It's going to be a lovely day. Your arrangements will be perfect. All the people will be there and that's the most important part—the people."

Mom patted LeeAnn's cheek. "That's lovely of you to say, but I need to follow-up on a few things."

LeeAnn dropped her arms and sighed. "Sure, Mom." Under her breath, she added, "Whatever makes you happy." She dug her car keys and driving gloves out of her coat pocket, then checked other pockets for her phone and wallet. Everything was present and accounted for.

A gust of wind slammed into the farmhouse, rattling the old windows in their frames.

"Jacques Corbeau was right. We're in for a heck of a winter." Jesper put on his coat, toque, and gloves.

Another blast of wind smacked the storm door against the wall when Mom went out, her head tucked like a turtle into her collar.

He waggled his eyebrows at LeeAnn, making her grimace at their made-up code for *This will all go away soon*. "C'mon, let's get you going." He stole another kiss, making her laugh.

She snuggled under his arm for the short trip to the car. As they crossed an icy patch, the wind buffeted them so hard they had trouble walking. Without the anchor of Jesper, LeeAnn would have sprawled on the ground several times. She opened the car doors and Mom climbed in, slamming the passenger door behind herself. Jesper pulled LeeAnn into a final hug and kiss. An impatient knocking on the car window ended the kiss long before LeeAnn was ready.

"Four more days, my love, and we'll never be interrupted again."

Smiling, LeeAnn slipped behind the wheel. The car purred to life, and they moved off down the long driveway, heading toward the road to Clarence Bay.

Once they left the shelter of the windbreak and crossed the open field lying dormant under a thick blanket of pristine snow, the car started to rock. Outside, the wind whipped hard pellets of snow across the field, blurring the scenery. The ancient white pine, a lone reminder of the logging days, bent in the onslaught of wind and snow. LeeAnn and her mom peered through the windshield. They exchanged anxious glances.

"Don't go over the shoulder, LeeAnn."

LeeAnn slowed for greater traction and control, fighting the steering wheel.

"We should turn back, Mom. It's too risky."

An eerie creaking and cracking noise brought the Ghost of Christmas Past to mind... except it wasn't clanking chains...

The big white pine leaned unnaturally far over the driveway.

LeeAnn gunned the engine, hitting black ice and skidding sideways instead of forward to safety. Crashing, screaming, shattering glass: an endless river of sound poured around them. A branch broke over the roof and stabbed through the windshield. LeeAnn shrieked, struggling out of her seatbelt, crawling over the console to shield her screaming mother. "Are you hurt?" she asked, but her words were lost in the ear-splitting cacophony. The jagged branch filled the car with the cheerful scent of Christmas. Soft, cold needles stroked the back of LeeAnn's neck. She screeched and arched away.

A deafening silence followed and stretched for seeming eternity.

"LeeAnn?" Mom cried, hysteria edging her words.

"Mom?" LeeAnn's voice quavered, small and uncertain.

"I'm here. Are you okay?" Mom replied.

LeeAnn sagged with relief. "Yes. No harm done. What about you?"

"Terrified out of my soul, but still here, still in one piece."

"Thank God. Can you get out?"

Mom tried the door. It opened a few centimetres and stopped. "No, what about you?"

LeeAnn's door wouldn't budge either. "Can you see either of our purses? We can call the house," she said.

Mom brushed her hands over her thighs, then peered around in the dark. "Mine was in my lap. You put yours in the back seat." She shuffled her feet around the foot well. "I can feel it, but I can't reach it because of the branch in the front window." She sighed. "LeeAnn honey, I think you might be able to squeeze out the window of your door."

LeeAnn assessed the situation. Mom's window was blocked with pine needles and small branches pressing against unbroken glass. Cautiously, she tried to lower her own window and was ridiculously happy when it buzzed down as if nothing was wrong. LeeAnn poked her head out and surveyed the area. A thick branch was jammed against the door. No wonder she hadn't been able to open it.

She manoeuvred herself out the window and perched on the door frame. She got one knee out and placed a booted foot on the branch and shoved. The branch screeched its way down the door panel and thumped onto the ground. LeeAnn levered her other leg out and hopped to the ground. A wide debris field of branches and needles circled the car. She tried the door again with no luck. The tree had done too much damage.

"Your turn, Mom."

"N-no, I couldn't. I won't fit through the window."

"C'mon, Mom, you can do it. Can you wiggle yourself into the driver's seat?"

"No. I'm too old for such nonsense." Still, Mom was doing it even as she was saying she couldn't.

LeeAnn hid a smile. When her dad had been alive, Mom had leaned on him for everything. Now that she was on her own, she still said "Oh, I couldn't possibly!" even while she took matters into her own hands. LeeAnn had even caught her watching a how-to video on fixing a loose deadbolt. She was learning how to rescue herself.

At last, Mom perched on the door frame, half in, half out but facing backwards. "Mom, you're gonna have to—" Through the web of needles, light bounced and steadied.

Jesper, frozen with fear, stopped in his tracks at the outer perimeter of the field of broken branches. The overpowering scent of pine whirled in the wind. His flashlight picked out the little red car huddled under the fallen white pine; a sizable branch broken through the windshield.

"Jesper?" LeeAnn's shout came loud and clear.

She was alive!

His knees wobbled in relief. A slap on his back from *Far* pushed him back into action, dodging under the bizarre canopy of a sideways tree.

In a narrow, mostly branch-free spot, LeeAnn pressed against the car, talking to her mom. Norah perched backwards on the driver's door frame with her arms stretched out over the car roof.

Briefly, Jesper scooped his love to his chest, hugging her hard. A ragged sob escaped him. She burrowed into him, her hard shiver tearing at his heart.

She pushed a little away from him, lifted her head and tipped it to one side. "Hey, you," she chirped, acting like she'd just had a little adventure and not experienced a near-death event.

"Excuse me?" A voice came from near his shoulder.

Jesper refocussed on his surroundings.

"Hello, Jesper. Once you've let go of my daughter, I do wish you would spare a moment to assist me," she said in an oddly formal way, sounding like the Queen asking for a refill of her teacup.

"Of course, Mrs. Hadley."

"Such a good boy."

Jesper stood behind his future mother-in-law, wrapped his arms under hers and clasped his own forearms. He leaned to take her weight and stepped backwards to give her room to land. As her feet cleared the window, she scrambled to find her footing. A deafening blast of the horn rent the night air. Jesper staggered at the unexpected sound and slammed against a branch that mercifully held.

"You may release me now, young man."

"Yes, ma'am."

Norah brushed off her coat and straightened her hat. "Would you please retrieve our purses and my briefcase, please? The wedding must still go on."

"Yes, ma'am." He exchanged perplexed glances with Lee-Ann. "Are you all right, ma'am?"

"I'm perfectly perfect." She paused, blinked, and looked around. "Or maybe not." She swayed for a moment before sliding toward the snow-covered ground.

"Your flashlight, please," LeeAnn demanded, holding out her mitten-covered hand. Once Jesper had passed it to her, she squatted down beside her mom. "Did you hit your head?" she asked, shining the light into her mother's eyes.

Norah batted the light away. "No, I—I'm just a little unsteady on my feet." She peered around her. "Or, apparently, *off* my feet."

Not willing to take her word for it, LeeAnn moved around her mom, using the flashlight to search her hair for bumps or, worse, blood.

A few minutes later, satisfied her mom was okay, given the circumstances, LeeAnn allowed Jesper to pull her to her feet. Then together, the young couple hauled Mrs. Hadley up, who promptly wrapped her arms around her daughter and began to sob.

LeeAnn hugged her back, eyes closed tight, chin wobbling. "I love you, too, Mom."

Feeling the need to burn off some adrenaline, Jesper threw his weight on the branch, causing the car to shake. Now knowing it wasn't going to shift and crush him, he reached into the little car, then handed over their purses and the all-important briefcase. The impact had shattered LeeAnn's phone. As the boughs cracked and swayed around them, they hunched over and walked clear of the fallen tree.

Far swept LeeAnn into a bear hug. "*Gud ske tak i himlen!*" he said, in a rare emotional slip into Danish to thank God in heaven. "Guess you're staying the night."

The wind toyed with their clothing as they trekked back up the hill to the farmhouse.

As they entered the foyer, the lights flickered and steadied. No sooner had they all sighed with relief than the lights flickered again. Only, this time, they stayed out.

Moments later, the sound of the generator filled the air, and a few designated lights came back on.

It looked like they were all here for the duration.

Three Days Before the Wedding

"Good morning, Tove," LeeAnn greeted her future mother-in-law.

"*Godt morgen*," Tove replied in Danish, then continued in slightly accented English. "What would you like for breakfast? You have a choice of bacon and eggs or porridge."

"A bowl of cold cereal?"

"Not at this table and not on a day when the house will get chilly with only two woodstoves to keep us warm. How does Red River hot cereal sound?"

"How did you know that's my favourite porridge?"

"Oh, I had a word with a not-so-little bird this morning." Tove's large hazel eyes twinkled at LeeAnn.

Stomping noises in the mudroom heralded the arrival of Jesper and his father, Erik. They hung up coats and hats and toed off heavy boots. Brisk cold air followed them into the kitchen. Erik gave Tove a quick kiss. "All's well in the barn. The goats are fed and watered, and the chickens and pigs are happy. The generator's all set with enough fuel for a week or so."

Jesper padded over and greeted LeeAnn with a kiss, only he took a little longer. She did love his kisses. LeeAnn shivered at the touch of Jesper's cold face in contrast to his warm arms. He rubbed his nose against her warm neck, making her scrunch her shoulders.

"You'll have to get used to chilly kisses as a farmer's wife," Tove said over her shoulder as she scooped the blend of grains into a pot, added water, raisins, and a pinch of salt.

"Make some for me, too, *Mor*? I'll have a second breakfast with my sweet fiancée," Jesper begged.

LeeAnn blushed at the teasing.

"Leave the girl be." Erik came to her defence.

She was so looking forward to living with this loving, laughing family. The plan was for Jesper's parents to move to one of the three bungalows on the property and leave the big farmhouse for her and oldest son Jesper. Jesper's two brothers lived in the other two bungalows.

"What on earth are you all laughing about? The radio said the power is out all over, and they don't know when it will be restored." Mom's fretful voice snuffed the joy in the room. For a long moment, the only sound was the cereal bubbling on the stove.

Erik left, muttering about records to update. Jesper kissed LeeAnn on the cheek and followed his father. Tove went back to her cooking. Mom gazed around the room as if she was wondering what had happened.

So much for sharing breakfast with her fiancé. LeeAnn sighed. Mom had become so querulous and fussy and… anxious… about everything since Dad had died three years ago. It was as if Mom hoped that total control could keep bad things from happening. Jesper had called her "Momzilla" once. LeeAnn had scolded him, even though she couldn't help but agree. The unflattering name came to mind again as Mom straightened every chair and swept up every crumb on the table before she sat down.

LeeAnn wondered if their near-death experience with the tree might affect her mom's behaviour—a you-only-live-once, make-the-best-of-it, go-with-the-flow kind of thing. She ran a hand through her still-damp hair. Guess not.

Tove dished up three bowls of hot cereal. She put two on a tray with spoons and three mugs of coffee. The other she placed in front of Mom.

Mom stared at the cooked cereal in horror. "That's far too heavy for breakfast. We'll have tea and toast. LeeAnn, why aren't you sitting down? It's better for your digestion if you sit down."

Tove handed the tray to LeeAnn. "Jesper will be waiting for you in the office, and Erik will want his coffee. You go eat with them."

LeeAnn glanced between her expectant mom and her mother-in-law-to-be. She always tried to be the dutiful daughter, but now she had two mothers… What's a bride to do?

Tove fluttered her hands. "Get away with you. I'll stay with Norah."

LeeAnn grinned and ran off, only too happy to be freed from her mother's demands. Behind her, Tove's calm voice reassured Mom that everything was under control.

In the office, LeeAnn distributed porridge and coffee, and settled down to enjoy her yummy breakfast.

Between mouthfuls, the men discussed ways and means to deal with the fallen tree. The rise and fall of their deep voices soothed LeeAnn's frazzled nerves.

On Saturday, four days from now, LeeAnn would finally marry her Jesper. And while she wanted to be his wife more than anything, she couldn't help admitting she was almost as anxious to get away from her mom.

"We have to cancel the wedding!" Norah's shriek tore into the quiet of the kitchen where Jesper, LeeAnn, and his parents discussed changes to the interior of the farmhouse.

Jesper jumped and spilled coffee down his blue checked flannel shirt. He gave her a foul look, which she ignored.

"Did you not hear me? I said we have to cancel the wedding and you're sitting like mannequins! Start phoning people! I've already called Louise about the flowers."

Jesper slanted a look at LeeAnn, who gave an excellent impression of a deer blinded by headlights. "Why?" he asked Norah.

"John's van broke down and the bird of paradise flowers won't be here on time."

"Okay. Can your sister-in-law make a bouquet using other flowers? Roses or something? She owns a flower shop, yes?" Jesper said.

Norah's lip curled in disgust. "She's already suggested that… I'm sure Louise can make all kinds of ordinary bouquets with ordinary flowers. But roses aren't good enough for my daughter's wedding. Don't you want LeeAnn's Special Day to be perfect?"

"It's my day, too." Jesper turned to his fiancée. She was getting that look on her face—the look that said she was about to cave, even though she really didn't want to. Slowly her expression changed to *Help me*. He gave her a reassuring smile and was relieved to see the tension eased from her sweet face.

"Mrs. Hadley. Norah. LeeAnn has waited… We've waited three years for our big day. I know you want everything to be perfect, but we knew when we planned a winter wedding that some things might not go as planned. The wedding is not cancelled. If the flowers don't arrive in time, I'm sure LeeAnn will be delighted with any bouquet made with her aunt's love." Jesper knew this because he and LeeAnn had discussed Norah's arrangements over and over and over again. "As long as we're together with our friends and families, the day will be special." He turned to his fiancée and held out his hand. "The important thing is getting married. Right, sweetheart?"

LeeAnn nodded. "It's not about the flowers, Mom." She clasped his hand and squared her shoulders. "Jesper's right. The important thing is that we get married, that we *are* married. We don't want to postpone it again. Once was enough."

Norah stiffened. "Do you mean to say you would have gone ahead with the wedding last time? With your father not even cold in his grave?"

Huh? Jesper shared a slack-jawed look with LeeAnn. She opened her mouth to speak, then clamped it shut. Muscles jumped in her cheeks. Jesper cringed at her visible effort to control herself. He was so glad he'd never pushed LeeAnn this far and would take great care never to do it in the future.

Her grip on his hand tightened. "Mom, please. We are getting married on Saturday, come hell or high water. If the flowers arrive on time, good. If not, I will be delighted with whatever Aunt Louise can do for me. If you find yourself too distressed over the flowers, then don't come."

"Well! I have never been spoken to like that in my life, young lady!"

It was about damn time. That's what he wanted to say to Momzilla. He supposed he should attempt to placate her, but he didn't want to upset LeeAnn's strategy—if she had one. They'd talked about Norah's control-freak ways and hadn't come up with an answer on how to deal with it. LeeAnn was hesitant to challenge Norah, fearing she'd drop back into the deep depression she'd suffered when her husband had died. LeeAnn felt that only the promise of a wedding and grandkids had eased it. Unfortunately, in the process, they'd created a monster.

Erik, silent and overlooked until now, stood to his full impressive height. He placed hands of support on LeeAnn's and Jesper's shoulders. "The wedding belongs to the children, and they have decided. Can you leave it be?"

Norah puffed. "Well, fine! If they want a less-than-perfect wedding, they're welcome to it." She scooped up her phone, then marched from the room and up the stairs. Moments later, the guest bedroom door slammed shut.

A snap from the fire in the woodstove broke the spell. Jesper added a couple more logs. "Thanks, *Far*. We owe you one."

"*Det var så lidt*," *Far* acknowledged before going back to the farm office with his coffee.

Jesper headed for the coffee pot that stayed on even with short power. Coffee was to Danes as tea was to Brits; good in any crisis.

LeeAnn looked up from where she busily stroked the kitchen table, seeking stray crumbs. She'd gathered quite a pile in front of herself.

Jesper sat beside her and ran a supportive hand down her back. "We're safe for now," he gave his mouth a wry twist.

LeeAnn nodded.

"It won't be long before she's back. There's no fireplace upstairs. The only heat is from passive air rising through the old grates."

LeeAnn nodded again.

"Did you mean it about uninviting your mom?"

LeeAnn shook her head. Tears pooled in her eyes.

"I didn't think so."

His small, teasing smile soothed her.

"She'll be back," he said.

"Of course. But I'm going to stand firm this time."

Across the table, Tove sighed. "She only wants the best for you."

"I know. Unfortunately, we have different opinions on what is *the best*. For me, the best is a backyard barbeque with all my family and friends, including kids under twelve, sharing the joy and excitement. I don't need a big swishy dress or a fancy, expensive bouquet. A little white dress and seasonal flowers are all I've ever wanted. And almost had three years ago. My poor dad." LeeAnn sighed heavily and leaned against Jesper's shoulder.

LeeAnn's phone chimed with an incoming call from her Aunt Louise. She put the phone on speaker.

"Hi, sweetie."

"Hi, what's up, Aunt Louise?"

"Your mother just called to cancel the wedding because your flowers are stuck in Toronto with your Uncle John."

LeeAnn frowned at Jesper. "Yeah, Mom told you before she told us."

"Are you good with that?"

"No, the wedding isn't cancelled. Please make a bouquet from whatever you have in stock. I know it will be beautiful."

"I'm glad to hear it." Aunt Louise paused. "Actually, Shelby wants to do your bouquet, a Christmassy one. Is that okay?"

A huge smile spread across LeeAnn's face. She flicked a questioning glance at Jesper who nodded his agreement. "That would be awesome. I've always loved Shelby's creations."

After everyone else had trooped upstairs to bed for the night, LeeAnn met Jesper in the sitting room. He straightened, getting up from stirring the fire and settled his hands at her waist.

"What's on your mind?" LeeAnn's soft hand rested against his cheek. She ran her thumb over his bottom lip.

Tingles ran down his spine. He wrapped his arms around her and tugged her close. "I've got you on my mind. You and the things I want to do with you."

She grinned and winked, slow and wicked.

Desire pulsed through him. He loved LeeAnn's wicked ways. The way she could turn him on, make him hot and eager, with only a look.

"Are you two coming upstairs?" *Mor's* voice burst their hot little bubble.

"Not yet, Tove." His fiancée's voice was so innocent, and her hand was so naughty. "Jesper and I want to chat a bit more."

A long pause ensued. "Well then, have fun."

LeeAnn placed a palm on his chest and walked him backwards until his knees hit the couch, until he was forced to sit. He shifted, trying to find space in his suddenly too tight jeans.

"You make yourself comfortable. I want some water." She leaned over and gave him a long, hard stroke that lifted his hips off the couch. She chuckled wickedly and he slumped back down. What a trickster.

His tricky love re-entered the room wearing nothing but woolly socks and an inviting smile. After pulling the pocket doors closed, she strolled across the room, her hips loose with an extra swing. "You have too many clothes on." She reached for his shirt buttons.

He spared a glance at the sliding doors that were closed but not locked. "What if…" His voice trailed off as LeeAnn tugged his shirt from his jeans, popped the button, and lowered the zipper. Lust stormed through him, blowing away all thought and leaving behind only sensation. When she climbed on top of him, settling down with him deep inside her, he groaned. She planted her hands on his shoulder and took him for a ride. A hard, fast, slick ride that left his heart straining to break free.

She settled her forehead on his shoulder, her breasts heaving against his chest. If he wasn't already spent, she would have driven him nuts.

Next time.

He ran his hands up and down her back, like she usually did for him, soothing and loving. She purred like he never did. The soft sound added to his satisfaction. Note to self… *LeeAnn is the boss in bed whenever she wants to be.* He smiled against her hair and hugged her tight. He drew the afghan over her cooling skin and earned another purr. Oh man, just the throaty sound against the side of his neck nearly got him going all over again.

Her purr turned into a chuckle. "Before we do it again, we need to talk."

Those four words were enough to kill any good mood.

She dismounted and pulled on enough clothes for decency. "You need to cover up."

Oh, man. Was she going to cancel the wedding for good? He was so scared stiff; he couldn't manage buttons.

"Is this about your mom?"

"Sort of."

"About my mom?"

"Kind of."

"My dad?"

"All of them and your brothers, too."

"Uh... the wedding?" He was completely stumped.

She paused for a moment. "Well, there are repercussions. It's connected to what we're doing, well did, just now."

"We made love... We haven't used protection on purpose." Clink, clank, clunk; the penny dropped. "You're pregnant?"

She nodded, beaming her biggest smile.

He opened and closed his mouth. He had no words. But he had plenty of hugs and kisses to give her.

She crowed with triumphant laughter.

"When did you find out? How did you find out?"

She grinned sheepishly. "I was carrying a test kit around until enough time had passed for an accurate result. I did it just now, when I was upstairs."

"Wait until we tell them tomorrow morning. They'll be so excited."

"No, you can't say a thing. Mom's already upset enough."

"You don't think she'll be happy about it?"

"Eventually. After we're married. Before we're married, she'll go ballistic. We'll tell her after the honeymoon."

Two Days Before the Wedding

The next morning, LeeAnn and Tove put the final touches on a big farmer's breakfast. Jesper, his dad and younger brothers, stomped into the mudroom. Their hearty masculine voices filled the kitchen with cheer as everyone settled around the table. The brothers, still single, had their own homes on the other side of the road that split the farm.

Quick footsteps clattering down the stairs warned of Mom's bustling entry into the kitchen. She sat at her place beside Lee-Ann, grinning from ear to ear, waving her phone around. "Now, we have to cancel the wedding. The highway is closed. Neither the caterer, the baker, nor the DJ can make it through. The caterer says they have a power failure in the city as well and he can't cook anything. Worse, they've had to eat the food he'd prepared for us because the grocery stores are closed."

LeeAnn stared at her mom's glowing triumph.

"Don't you understand? Now we have the chance to make the wedding bigger and better!"

Rigid with anger, LeeAnn shot from her chair. "No! I don't want bigger or better. I want to get married on Saturday."

"You can't get married without flowers or food or music," Mom replied.

"Why not?"

"It's unheard of."

"So?"

"So, I forbid it!"

LeeAnn's jaw dropped. "Who *are* you?"

Mom reared back. "I'm your mother."

"You're not the mother I had three years ago."

"Three years ago, I had a husband who respected my choices. I had a daughter who didn't rebel at every turn. I had a calm and happy life. And now it's all gone," Mom continued with a catch in her voice. "I want to give my daughter the perfect wedding. But because of some stupid freak-of-the-century ice storm, it can't happen. All I want is to give you the wedding of our— your—dreams." Mom deflated as her rant ended. She tossed her phone onto the table.

Tove reached across the table and tapped Mom's hand to get her attention. "Why do *you* want it so badly, Norah?"

"I just want the best for my only daughter. Is that so bad?" Mom was so bewildered. All her life she'd lived by the motto "Only the Best is Good Enough". She seemed stunned her daughter didn't share her conviction.

"Sometimes, the best choice isn't the right choice. Sometimes your idea of the best isn't what others want for themselves. Sometimes, you have to let others choose for themselves."

"Then *why* did you agree with all my decisions?" Mom fired back.

Jesper squeezed LeeAnn's hand, lending her his strength.

"Because it cheered you up so much, I couldn't say no. I couldn't handle the guilt if I made you sad again."

"We can have Chloe shorten the dress for the next wedding. What do you think? Third time lucky?" Mom coaxed, carrying on as LeeAnn hadn't spoken.

LeeAnn sat back and gawped at Mom. "Seriously? Schedule three weddings to the *same man*?"

"Don't look at me like that, young lady." Mom wagged a finger at her. "How can you have a wedding without flowers, food, a cake, music, a venue, and a dress? Don't let stubbornness make you illogical."

"The power could come back any second."

"The power company says the entire province is out."

"That doesn't mean it won't come back. Remember how it did the same thing a few summers ago."

"You still won't have flowers, food, a cake, or music."

"I have flowers," LeeAnn said. "Aunt Louise called and offered a bouquet made by Shelby."

Before Mom could draw enough breath for a rant, Tove raised her hand. "May I say something?"

Mom nodded. So did LeeAnn, expecting her future mother-in-law to be on her side.

"LeeAnn, *min kære*, maybe your mother is right. Think of how hard it would be to find substitutes for everything. I'm sure Shelby could do up a bouquet in time, but all the other things...? You have flowers you'll love and a dress you don't like. You could do without music." She waved her arm over the table crowded with serving dishes. "But food? Do you really want your friends and family to sit down to an empty table?"

The stubbornness holding LeeAnn upright seeped away. Slumping in her chair, she surrendered. There would be no wedding. Again.

The clatter of dishes in the big kitchen battered LeeAnn's ears. She passed the bowl of home fries from Jesper to Mom without taking any.

"Are you sure you don't want any?" Mom said.

"No, thanks. I'm not hungry."

"Tove went to a lot of trouble." Mom tipped the bowl suggestively.

"Leave her be, Norah," Jesper said from LeeAnn's other side. "She needs to keep up her strength."

"She's plenty strong."

LeeAnn stared from one person to the other. When had she become a prize to be fought over? Her appetite gone, LeeAnn excused herself from the table. She wandered into the living room, wrapped a cheerful daisy-patterned afghan around herself and dropped into the rocker, setting it in motion.

Was she ever going to marry Jesper? Twice now, the fates had conspired against her. Next time? Next time, she promised herself, she was going to do it *her* way.

And no time like the present to start a new plan. She needed some paper and a pen. She scanned the room. Where did Tove keep such stuff? The side table? The coffee table drawer? There. She smoothed the paper and titled it "Wedding #3".

It had to be soon, or they'd have more to worry about than her fitting into her dress. The new date would be Valentine's Day. LeeAnn smiled to herself at the memories Jesper had given her of that day. Shelby would make a bouquet of seasonal flowers, maybe silk tulips to last forever. Ryan would create an awesome Québécois feast; duck *confit, tourtiéres, crêpes Suzette, clafoutis*. Some barbeque, of course. Barbeque in the winter? Why the heck not? And don't forget the chocolate cake. Yum. Carlotta would play the piano for the ceremony and Julia would sing at the reception. Chloe would shorten the dress.

It would be a casual affair, focussed on the important things—the love she and Jesper shared, and the love they shared with their family and friends. Mom could like it or lump it. She didn't have to come. LeeAnn didn't need her mom to walk her down the aisle. Shelby's dad would be happy to do it. Heck, she could walk herself down the aisle—marking the transition from daughter to wife. Underline that. And Pachelbel's "Canon in D" for the processional.

Resentful triumph burned in LeeAnn's chest. She thumped the arm of the rocker. Her wedding was *her* wedding, not her mother's. No more of this pushover nonsense. Nothing was going to stop her… Them.

She sat back to review her list. A wave of bleak hopelessness drowned her triumph. "Who am I kidding? Our child will graduate before Mom accepts this." She scored an angry X across the list, tore the page from the pad, scrunched it up and threw it into the fire. The dead fire. Grrrr!

LeeAnn rose from her seat, snatched the stupid paper from the stupid ashes, marched through the kitchen, and threw the pointless list in the garbage can under the sink. She stuffed herself into her jacket and boots. "I'm going for a walk," she barked at Jesper and Tove, who stood gaping at her.

Outside, a blast of ice-cold wind cut through LeeAnn. This was no place for human nor beast. She headed to the barn; the goats and their kids were always good for a laugh.

Jesper turned to his mom, speaking in Danish, "Why is she so mad?"

Tove straightened from the garbage bin with LeeAnn's crumpled paper in her hand. "This might explain it."

Jesper took the lined notepaper from *Mor* and smoothed it out. As he read, he smiled. "This is her plan for our next wedding. But she put a big X through it all. Why?"

"My guess is something to do with Norah. Don't let that list out of your sight," *Mor* said.

"Good advice." He tucked it neatly in his shirt pocket for future reference. Through the window, Jesper spotted a sad figure slipping into the barn. LeeAnn had gone to the goats. Another smile tugged at his mouth. His fiancée had always had an affection for the critters.

Mor touched his arm, drawing his attention back. "Go to her. Cheer her up."

"It's not her fault the fates have a grudge against us."

"Perhaps they are challenging the two of you, instead."

"Why? Isn't she sweet enough already?" He ignored the reference to himself.

"*Ja*, very sweet. She's done so many things for others. Perhaps it's time someone did something for her."

Jesper nodded; *Mor* had a strong point.

"Go on, now. She needs you."

"*Mange tak, Mor.*" He kissed his mom's cheek and headed out to the barn.

He slipped in quietly and strolled down the aisle to the large hay-filled pen. Along the way, he checked on the chickens.

LeeAnn's voice came from further down the large barn. Who was she talking to? He peeked around the enormous stack of hay, seeing his beloved sitting forlornly on a straw bale. Was she actually having a chat with a goat?

"You know, Tinker, my mom could give you and your herd lessons in stubborn."

The goat bleated in reply.

Laughter rippled in Jesper's chest. At least LeeAnn had chosen the herd's matriarch to consult. If anyone understood stubborn, it would be Tinker.

"I'm such a pushover. I hate that about myself," she told the goat. "I'm not shy or anything. I just have trouble 'setting boundaries.'"

Jesper could hear the quotations marks around the trendy phrase. He stopped. He knew he should announce himself, but he really wanted to hear what LeeAnn had to say. It wasn't as if Tinker would spill the beans later.

"But I can't help myself. After Dad died, Mom was so sad, so closed down." Jesper's heart twisted to hear her voice break. Tinker lightly butted her shoulder as if to tell her to buck up. LeeAnn gave a watery chuckle and rubbed the goat's head. "I wish somebody, anybody, would nudge things along so Jesper and I can get married. I want to move on with our lives instead of always having to wait. You don't happen to have a wedding miracle in your pocket, eh, Tinker? Of course not, no pockets."

LeeAnn's soft sob broke Jesper's heart. Why hadn't he noticed this before? *Mor* was right. LeeAnn gave and gave endlessly to the people she loved. Everyone was, of course, suitably grateful, but LeeAnn *never* expected or asked for anything in return.

Guilt poured through him. He was just as bad. Shame added to his burden of guilt. He often took too much from his generous love and didn't give back anywhere near enough. Oh sure, he gave her flowers and small gifts... But, on the whole, he was an ungrateful asshole.

He had to do something.

But what?

He tapped his shirt pocket where LeeAnn's list was tucked away. Was he nuts? Probably. Could he pull it off? Possibly. Would Momzilla agree? Or give it all away? He had no idea. But come hell or high water—or another ice storm, LeeAnn would have her wedding on Saturday. Jesper, with a little help from LeeAnn's friends and family, would make it happen. He backed into the barn's depths and pulled out his phone. Luckily, he had some power and enough bars. He'd have to talk fast, because he couldn't go to the house and risk nosy Norah overhearing him. And he'd better avoid LeeAnn, because she would sense his secret in a heartbeat.

His last call ended with a dead battery and a stunned heart. Everyone had a tale to tell of how much LeeAnn meant to them, and they'd gladly offered to do whatever he asked. He was deeply humbled. Why had he never heard these stories before? He knew LeeAnn gave with grace, never bragging about her deeds. But this much? Hell, she'd save Tyler's life! He was marrying a genuine angel.

One Day Before the Wedding

"So will you do it, *Mor*?" Jesper had laid out his plans to Mor when they met in the kitchen the next morning after chores. Power or not, the farm still needed tending from dawn to dusk.

She beamed up at him. "*Ja*, I will. We all will. But what about Norah?"

"What about me?" Norah demanded from the doorway into the hall.

Jesper squared his shoulders and turned to greet the one stumbling block in his plan. Correction, not the only block, just the biggest one. The others were more manageable.

"I need your help," he said.

"Of course. How can I help you?" She seated herself at the table.

"Well, it's more your daughter you'll be helping."

Alarm pinched her features. "LeeAnn? What's wrong? Is she okay? I thought she was still in bed…"

"It's not an emergency, but it is desperate."

"Hear him out, Norah. He has a plan," *Mor* said, throwing in her support.

"LeeAnn and I are getting married tomorrow, and I need your help to make it happen."

"I beg your pardon?"

He sighed; knowing it was going to be tough. "LeeAnn and I—"

She waved a dismissive hand. "I heard you. But apparently, you haven't heard that the wedding was cancelled. We have no flowers, no food, no music, and no dress… Therefore, no wedding. It's hardly my fault, but I did what needed to be done… I made the calls myself."

"I made some calls, too. The wedding is back on. Tomorrow at four o'clock at the Festival Hall."

"It's what?" She was cold and stiff now, colder and stiffer than usual. "It can't be. We have no flowers, no music—"

"Don't worry about that, Norah," *Mor* piped up. "Jesper's taken care of everything."

"You know about this, Tove?" Norah stared at her hostess. "Why didn't anyone tell me? I've made all these phone calls only to have you tell everyone to ignore me. People must think I'm an idiot who doesn't know what is going on in her own daughter's life. I feel like a fool." She started to cry.

"I only found out just now, Norah," *Mor* replied in a soothing voice.

Norah turned back to Jesper. "You spoke to *her*? I guess my opinion doesn't matter then. After all, I'm *only* the Mother of the Bride."

"Yes, you are. And *Mor* is the Mother of the Groom… me." He shook his head at the sheer lameness of his statement. "I share things with my mom." He sighed. "Back to the point. I've arranged for everything to be at the Hall for our four o'clock wedding on Saturday." He held up his hand in classic stop-sign mode. "Please listen before you condemn my plan."

If she was stiff before, she now turned to granite.

"I want to give LeeAnn what she wants. That's your goal, too. Perhaps, you've been a little too self-absorbed to notice that

LeeAnn has gone along with whatever you want because she loves you, and she's worried about you. That's the way she's built."

Norah blinked.

He struggled on. "LeeAnn is a giver. Right?"

Norah's chin dipped a few millimeters.

She gives and gives, and everyone—you, me, *Mor*—we love her for it. Right?"

Norah tipped her head, listening.

"So a group of us have decided it's time to give back. LeeAnn has never before said 'I want'. So when she finally says she wants something, I want to make sure we give it to her." He held out his hand. "Will her only family work with us?"

A long moment passed with agonizing slowness.

Norah stared at his hand. She pulled her own hands off the table to her lap.

He dropped his hand and sighed from the bottom of his soul. It was time to bring out the big guns. He pulled LeeAnn's list form his shirt pocket, smoothed it out, and laid it in the middle of the table. "You won't help us? You won't give back to your daughter in the way *she* wants rather than the way *you* want?"

Wounded and suspicious, Norah placed a single finger on the crumpled page and dragged it a bit closer. She scanned the list, in LeeAnn's handwriting, of what her daughter wanted for Wedding #3. Her mouth pulled into a hard line. "Is this where you got the idea to call some friends and force them to provide a wedding in the middle of a widespread power failure?"

He ignored the part about forcing; they'd all been delighted to do something for LeeAnn. "That list is proof of what Lee-Ann—*The Bride*—wants."

Norah pushed the paper to one side. "If this is what LeeAnn wants, why did she agree to everything I suggested?"

This again. "Uh…." He knew why, but he couldn't find the words with the right degree of delicacy. He threw a pleading look to *Mor.*

She gave a brisk nod. "She told you, but you weren't listening. She did what you wanted, because she was afraid to upset you again once you started to feel better."

Norah took her time thinking. "You mean she felt sorry for me? Her lonely, widowed mother?" Norah twisted her hands around each other, then nodded and let out a long sigh. "It's true. I was deeply depressed after my Don died so suddenly. I couldn't make life work without him. When you and LeeAnn started planning your second wedding, it pulled me out of my blue mood, and gave me something happy to think about." Her chin wobbled and firmed. "But instead of helping my dear girl, I turned into Momzilla. Yes, I heard you earlier, Jesper."

Jesper's cheeks burned with embarrassment.

"You see, I was so afraid…" Tears welled in Norah's eyes. She dropped her gaze to her hands beneath the table. Jesper could picture them twisting until the knuckles whitened.

Mor moved around the table to take the seat beside Norah and wrapped a careful arm over Norah's shoulders. "Afraid of what, *min kære?*"

"I was afraid that—" She swallowed hard. "I was afraid that LeeAnn wouldn't come visit me… That she'd be too busy with her new life with Jesper and your family. And if that happened… I'd truly be left alone." With those blurted words, Norah clamped both hands over her mouth, fighting for composure.

Mor clasped Norah tighter to her side. "Norah, *nej,* we couldn't do that if we tried. LeeAnn wouldn't let us. She loves you and we love her. You will always be welcome in our home, no invitation needed."

Norah nodded, brushed aside her tears, and heaved another great sigh. She stood, then squared her shoulders, took her daughter's list, and left the room.

Jesper exchanged a questioning glance with *Mor.* What had they done?

The Wedding Day is Here

Early the next morning, Jesper and *Far* were stomping into their boots getting ready for chores. *Mor* was at the stove as usual.

Norah entered the room, disheveled from sleep. "Okay, I'll do it. I've been thinking about it all night. I've been a huge pain. How can I help? Are all the arrangements set? Is everyone on board with your crazy idea?"

"Everything's set. The only thing we need is an excuse to lure LeeAnn to the Hall and I have to somehow get my suit down there without her seeing." He didn't tell her he hadn't heard back from anyone. He tamped down the nerves screwing around in his stomach.

"And what about our dresses and your father's suit?"

"Uh…" Jesper looked to *Mor* for help.

"We'll go to town in separate trucks, and you can pick up your things on the way."

The sound of the generator starting up tore through the silent morning. Norah stared out the window at the sunshine. "I think we need another power failure." A loud bang from outside rattled the kitchen windows. They all jumped out of their skins then stared at each other with gaping mouths.

Far laughed heartily in the ensuing silence. *"Gud ske tak i himlen,* Norah! The Christmas Spirit was listening and gave us our reason!"

Upstairs, LeeAnn rolled over in her bed and stared out the window. How dare the sky be so cheerful and blue today, on her wedding day that wasn't. The sound of the generator starting up reminded her of the cause of her misery. How dare the rain freeze into ice? All of Mom's fretting and fussing hadn't covered this scenario.

Was Fate trying to tell her she shouldn't marry Jesper? Shortly before their first wedding, Dad had died from a massive heart attack. This time the whole town was without power. What next? A plague of locusts?

A loud bang from outside startled LeeAnn out of her morose thoughts. "What the heck was that?" She climbed out of her twin bed and shivered her way to the window, past the other very rumpled bed where Mom had slept last night.

Black smoke curled up from the generator in the shelter of the big farmhouse. The last fragile thread of electricity had snapped. They'd be huddling by the woodstoves today and squinting by candlelight tonight. What a marvellous day her wedding day was. Not!

LeeAnn pulled on chilly clothes and headed down to the kitchen. Mom and Tove fell silent as LeeAnn entered.

"What happened, Tove?"

"The generator blew. We don't have power for the well pump, so we have no water. We'll have to evacuate to the Festival Hall in town. They're open as a shelter."

Oh, joy. The Fates were rubbing salt into her failed wedding wound; the Hall was where her wedding should have been held.

"Is there enough water for coffee?"

"I'd just made a pot and some more cinnamon French toast. Sit and eat while I pack. We're bringing what food we can to help feed people at the Hall."

"Are you sure I can't help?"

"Absolutely. Norah and I will deal with everything. You have your breakfast. If they haven't sanded and salted the roads, it might be a long ride to town. While we're there, Erik and I will take your mom to your place so you can get some clean clothes."

LeeAnn sat and ate. At least she got her favourite breakfast.

Later, Erik, Tove, and Mom led the convoy. LeeAnn hopped into Jesper's truck. Jesper's older brother, Laurids, who would have been his best man, brought up the rear. The youngest brother, Jens, stayed with the animals. They loaded the trucks with food, a few cots, and a stack of blankets. The farmers had moved LeeAnn's little red car and cleared the large branches, but the still remaining debris made driving hazardous. The drivers edged cautiously around the remains of the fallen tree.

LeeAnn peered across the truck at Jesper. Something was going on with him. His left leg bounced, and he tapped the steering wheel in a frenetic rhythm.

"What are you up to?"

Jesper smiled back, all innocence. "Nothing. Nothing at all."

She crossed her arms and gave him a look of extreme doubt.

He shifted about guiltily but said nothing.

"Hmm."

"Well... I was desperate to escape from your mom."

She gasped in outrage then laughed because, really, she was with him on that point. Mom had been pretty unbearable during the whole wedding planning. The only consolation to having her second wedding postponed was to have the third wedding done her way. Good grief! Three weddings! She ran her hand up Jesper's thigh and got a quick intake of breath for her reward.

"LeeAnn," he warned. "I'm driving here."

She laughed and folded her hands demurely in her lap. "I'll be good... for now."

As they rolled slowly down the rural highway, the beauty silenced them. Ice coated everything; the landscape glistened in the sunlight. LeeAnn dug out Jesper's sunglasses from the glove box and pulled hers from her purse. At a curve in the road, tree branches met overhead in a crystal canopy. An open field blinded them with sparkles. The Hansen kids were skating everywhere on the ice, overjoyed at finding the biggest rink ever. Further down the road, kids had constructed a death-defying toboggan run. She shook her head. Life went on, even if her wedding wouldn't.

"Mind if we stop at the Nielsens?" Jesper asked. "I'd like to talk to Rob about helping Jens with the animals. We'll catch up with the others at the Hall."

"Sure. It'll be nice to have a short visit with them."

A couple of hours later, they were back on the road amazed at the sight of trees bent under the weight of beautiful, dangerous ice. The tires hummed across an almost bare stretch of road where little snow had penetrated the dense forest. Deer scattered out of a clearing where some kind person had dropped a few bales of hay. A small grove lay shattered by freezing from the inside out.

LeeAnn surreptitiously wiped a tear from her cheek.

"What's up, honey?" He laid a warm hand briefly on her thigh before returning it to the steering wheel.

"Nothing."

"Not buying it."

"Okay. I'm crying because there's so much beauty and so much devastation at the same time."

"And…"

She heaved a sigh. "And I still want to get married today. I'm being completely selfish when so many people are having such a hard time. But I can't help wishing for it, anyway."

"Aw, honey. If there had been any way to make it happen, you know I would have done it, right?"

"Do you think the minister will be around?"

"That's a great idea. But do you really want to get married in a snowsuit?"

She laughed at the image his words conjured. "No, I guess not."

Braking gently, Jesper coasted on ice, coming to a stop just a meter from a tree across the road. Fresh-sawn logs filled the ditches on either side. "Looks like *Far* and Laurids were here first, but another tree decided to screw with us. Good thing I brought a chain saw." Jesper turned off the engine, climbed out and made short work of clearing the road.

They passed the Jorgensen place. Smoke rose from the chimneys and a light was on, signalling all was good at their farm.

Jesper seemed to get more tense, more jittery, with each kilometer driven.

What was up with him?

At long last, they reached the main highway. Two tracks, precisely where the tires would go, straddled the dotted centre line. Between them lay a flat strip of snow. Jesper was tempted to pick up speed and whistle down the highway. But he knew better. Black ice, a thin sheet of invisible ice on the asphalt, had caused far too many moments of terror and often ended in grief. So the trip to town took far longer than usual.

Which gave LeeAnn a lot of time to assess the damage bordering the highway.

Once in town, the tree fall damage multiplied. Cars were crushed, outbuildings destroyed. Everything wore a top hat of two feet of snow covered by a glistening layer of ice. Few cars were about and even fewer people. Businesses were dark. Smoke rose from many chimneys—most people up here had wood-stoves, if not generators. This wasn't their first polar rodeo. In a dip in the terrain, a thin grey pall hung in the air, fumes from all the generators.

"Sheesh, it's kinda post-apocalyptic," LeeAnn said.

Jesper chuckled. "Beware zombies."

Giggling, LeeAnn waved away his warning. "*Pfft*, they couldn't stand the cold."

"Can't beat a rough and tough Canadian, eh?"

"Nah. Do you think zombies can ski?"

"The skis wouldn't stick to rotting flesh."

"Maybe the yellow snow will take care of them."

They were snorting with laughter as they arrived at the Festival Hall at a quarter after three. Light flowed from the lobby's wall of glass. Inside, people milled about in groups, while kids ran about in small hoards. LeeAnn's spirits lifted at the sight of her friends. Someone peered out and waved a greeting. Christmas decorations sparkled in the light.

Jesper's arm settled over her shoulders. "We'll have our wedding yet, my love."

She leaned against his warm and solid strength. "It's just that…"

"I wanted our wedding today, too. It's going to be lonely in our farmhouse on the hill."

For his sweet words, he got a kiss that fogged the windows.

A sharp rap on the truck window had them springing apart with guilty laughs.

"C'mon, Jesper, you've delayed long enough. Let's get this show on the road." His brother pointed his thumb at the Hall.

"Show? What show"? LeeAnn asked Jesper. Did he look guilty?

"The unloading of the extra food and stuff we brought. How would you like barbequed ribs for supper tonight?"

"Yum, my favourite." It's what she'd put on her new wedding list. LeeAnn climbed out of the truck.

"You go on in. Laurids and I will unload."

LeeAnn pushed down her regrets for another postponed wedding. The third time would be the charm. She and Jesper would be married on Valentine's Day with provisional planning for anything, including power failure. She'd been such a doormat, but—she was determined now. There would be no more caving to Mom, no matter what. She brushed a hand over her tummy, hoping she wouldn't be showing too much in two more months. Pushing through the front doors, the noise was deafening compared to the near-twilight stillness outside. The heat was tropical, and the energy level astonishing. Where had all these people come from?

A buzz whooshed around the vast space when first one person, then another noticed her arrival. Their reaction to her failed wedding made things so much worse. At least Jesper was still around, and she hadn't been dumped at the altar. She unzipped her parka and slid it off. Clomping over to the coat racks, she stepped out of her Kodiaks and into the slippers she'd brought from Jesper's place.

Whispers echoed through the massive open space.

Before LeeAnn could force herself to grin and bear the gossip, her cousin Shelby bustled over, wrapped an arm around her shoulders and led her to the stairwell.

"Shel, where are we going?" LeeAnn asked.

"You'll see."

Emerging one flight lower, Shelby tugged her along a hall lined with closed doors. They stopped in front of a door with a nameplate that read R.J. Barker, Manager.

LeeAnn pulled against Shelby's grip. "Does Reg want to speak to me about payment for a wedding that isn't happening? That's… I don't know what that is!"

"Nope. That's not why we're here." Shelby was grinning like a fool.

LeeAnn scowled at her cousin. "What are you up to?"

"This!" Shelby opened the door to reveal an office that wasn't an office. Instead, it was more like a classy room at a high-end hotel.

Well, not quite.

A mattress lay directly on the carpet, graced by a rich red and cream brocade coverlet. A gauzy canopy, ornamented with ribbons and silk flowers, hung from the ceiling and draped onto the floor. A gorgeous wedding dress hung on a hanger hooked over the closet door. *Wait a sec. Reverse.* The dress was her dress… but… shorter? A wonderful winter bouquet, an opened bottle of champagne, and several flutes rested on a large desk against a grey wall.

Shelby nudged LeeAnn into the room and shut the door behind them. "Welcome to your bridal boudoir." She giggled.

LeeAnn stared at Shelby. Her heart began to beat harder. Was this…? How could…?

Mom, dressed in her mother-of-the-bride finery, came through a door in the corner and swept her arm towards the room behind her. "Your bath awaits, my dear."

LeeAnn's eyes widened. "Who are you, and what have you done with my mother?"

Mom smiled sheepishly. "Yes, I am your mother. Your very apologetic mother. I'm sorry I didn't see what I was doing to you and Jesper. I'm sorry I burdened you with making me happy."

"Oh, Mom." Her voice wobbled as she gazed around the room, the dress, the flowers. "You made all these arrangements so Jesper and I can be married today?" Her fluttering hands rose to her mouth, tears filling her eyes.

Mom shared a glance with Shelby. "I had nothing to do with it. Jesper arranged it all with the help of your cousins and your friends. They all did this out of love for you. That man of yours is a hero." Mom heaved a sigh, then clapped her hands briskly. "Now, come along, honey, timed to get cleaned up."

Shelby planted her hands on LeeAnn's shoulders and gently shoved her into the bathroom. "I went to the house and got your special toiletry basket." Shelby gestured to the basket of goodies on the counter. "You've got thirty minutes. Go!"

Twenty-seven minutes later, LeeAnn was buffed and polished and smelled like a rose. Nine minutes later, Mom zipped up her wedding dress, and LeeAnn stepped into her shoes.

"The dress is awesome." LeeAnn fluffed out the short skirt of her dress. What an interesting movement in the fabric. How had Chloe done that? It was so cool. Speaking of which… "Where's Chloe, my other dear friend and bridesmaid?"

"In the hospital with baby Adam and hubby Seth. They had the baby at home. I don't have all the details, but everybody's safe and healthy. Obviously, they won't be here."

LeeAnn grinned. "I'm so happy for them!"

"That's wonderful. Chloe was so fretful, poor thing." Norah added her own joy to the announcement. "Seth must have been so relieved he could be with her."

LeeAnn paused, then waved a pointed finger at Shelby. "Something's wrong here. Where is your wedding outfit? I can't walk down the aisle without you."

"Oh, I totally forgot!" Shelby hurried to the closet, whipped out her classy blue dress, whizzed into the washroom, and out again at breath-taking speed. She ended with a flashy spin in front of LeeAnn. "Does the bride approve?"

LeeAnn giggled at her cousin. "The bride absolutely approves. You're gorgeous."

Shelby handed her the bouquet. "It's not as beautiful as you are, but then, nothing would be."

LeeAnn turned the arrangement in her hands, looking at each component. "It's amazing." She stroked a fingertip along a thin, twisty branch. "Where did you find all these things?"

Shelby shrugged. "Here, there, everywhere. Along the trail in town, special-order stock in the store, my imagination."

"It's the best, most beautiful bouquet I could have wished for. You're a wonder!" LeeAnn touched the tiny gift tucked amongst the silk poinsettias. "Is this real or a decoration?"

"It's real, a little something for you to open after the wedding," Shelby replied.

"Thank you!"

"Oh no," Mom stood stock still, her hand over her heart.

Fear gripped LeeAnn as she ran to her, and grabbed her by the shoulders, ready to catch her if she fell. This couldn't be a repeat of Dad's heart attack! "Mom! What's wrong? Are you okay?"

"Good grief! How could we forget?" She stared in horror at the two younger women.

"What?"

"Who?"

"We forgot the photographer!" She thrust up her hands in a gesture of frustration. "That's what happens when you leave it to a man to organize!"

LeeAnn gaped at Mom. "Huh?"

"We forgot about the photographer." Mom said every word as its own sentence.

LeeAnn sagged in relief. "Oh. Is that all?"

Mom thrust a finger into the air. "But… I have a solution." She hustled to the door. "Be right back. Don't start without me."

LeeAnn and Shelby stared at each other. "Is your mom losing it?"

LeeAnn shrugged. "Good question."

A few minutes later, Mom was back with Melody and Hayley in tow, their cameras at the ready. "I found the best photographers in the house! Between a reporter and a photographer's protégée, you'll have the best wedding pictures ever taken… or at least the most interesting." She tugged LeeAnn into position against the granite wall and gestured at the rather stunned photographers. "Well... Take pictures!"

Melody snapped out of her trance first. "Yes, ma'am. Can we have you to the left of LeeAnn and Shelby to the right?"

The photographers took turns capturing shared moments with LeeAnn's mom and cousin. When they were done, the two women returned to the auditorium, giving the bridal party a short time to catch their collective breath.

"Just one more point on procedure, sweetheart."

LeeAnn's heart sank, taking her patience with it. "What now, Mom?" She stared longingly into the hallway; so near and yet so far.

"Julia will me escort me down the aisle by myself. Shelby will precede you down the aisle, and you'll walk to Jesper on your own to symbolize your transition from daughter to wife." She paused. "Did I remember that right?"

LeeAnn gazed into her mom's teary eyes. "You read my notes."

"Jesper made me. Like I said, he masterminded the whole day just for you."

"Oh, Mom." LeeAnn wrapped her mom in a warm hug.

In sync, mother and daughter blinked rapidly, gusted sighs, and regained their control.

Shelby sniffled. "You two are making me cry." She waggled her phone and tapped out a message, "Meanwhile, the show must go on."

Moments later, a knock on the door had Shelby hopping up to open it.

"Julia!" LeeAnn rushed forward and swept her friend into a hug. "What are you doing here?"

"At the moment, I'm here to get you upstairs. Later, I'll be singing."

"Singing? Did Jesper ask you?"

"Yes. I've got your first dance all practiced up and ready to go… and we have a guest trio for a divine evening of dancing afterwards."

"Trio? Your accompanist, I presume, and who else?" Julia's grin confused LeeAnn.

"Alex is stuck in Toronto, so Carlotta is joining me—"

"But Carlotta doesn't do jazz." LeeAnn popped her hands onto her hips. "Un-confuse me, please."

"Have you ever heard of Marshall Rickerts and the Quâtre Jazz Quartet?"

LeeAnn thought a moment, then shook her head. "Nope."

"Didn't think so. Anyway, long story short, he happened to be in Clarence Bay. He's a friend of Carlotta's, and they've agreed to form a trio with me. Just for tonight. Just for you."

Shelby nudged LeeAnn from behind. "Please follow your wedding planner *du jour*."

The bridal party followed Julia upstairs to the empty foyer and stopped at one side of the closed auditorium doors. Julia slipped through them; in moments, all went quiet inside. Softly, the sound of a piano filtered through. Julia came to escort Mom to her seat. Shelby took her place in front of LeeAnn.

The doors opened and LeeAnn's jaw dropped. Candlelight flickered along the aisle and throughout a room flooded by a glorious sunset of pink and orange hues.

Beaming a huge smile, Julia waved her arms conductor-style. Pachelbel's "Canon in D" flowed out to greet them. LeeAnn gasped. It wasn't Mendelsohn as she'd expected. She exchanged a glance with Mom.

After the first bar, the audience rose from their seats and Julia nudged Shelby down the aisle to stand at the front of the room.

LeeAnn began her solo walk down the aisle. Her gaze touched on the smiling faces of family and friends on both sides. Melody snapped photos. Aunt Louise blew her a kiss. Friends and neighbours all showed their happiness to be with her on her special day. Mom wiped tears from her cheeks. Most attendees were dressed in jeans and casual gear, though a few had run home to hunt up fancy wear.

At the front of the room, Jesper waited, all decked out in his dark grey suit topped with his just-for-her smile. His love for her shone in his eyes.

Laurids poked Jesper in the ribs and murmured, "You are one lucky dude."

His throat tight with emotion, Jesper could only manage a nod. The world narrowed down to his beautiful bride with her just-for-him smile. He didn't notice the details of her dress or the flowers, only her beauty. Her joy reached inside him and ignited his own joy.

At last, she would be his, and he would be hers. At last, the little bean hidden behind her bouquet would be theirs. And last, he promised to give her back everything she gave him: coffee in the morning, tea in the evening, hugs and kisses and love all day long.

But first, they had to officially tie the knot. Carlotta finished the canon with a fanfare of notes and a huge smile.

"Dearly beloved…" the minister began. In the blink of an eye, the ceremony was over. No one objected, and their signatures were added to the documents, uniting two-and-a-bit people into one loving family.

Julia waved the newlyweds down the aisle and into the foyer, followed by the attendees. The auditorium doors were barely closed before volunteers rushed in, noisily shuffling chairs and rolling in tables, turning their chapel into a dining hall. Heavenly smells wafted into the foyer.

LeeAnn gasped at the selection of appetizers carried in on trays flowing from the kitchen. Tiny seafood tarts, miniature Vietnamese spring rolls, crunchy fresh veggies with dipping sauce— all her favourite appetizers—presented by all sorts of people in all sorts of casual gear. LeeAnn gazed up at her grinning groom. "You've been a very busy man, my husband. Have I told you lately that you're my hero."

"I just made a few phone calls, my wife. You're the real hero."

"Those must have been some calls…" He gave her only a mischievous wink in reply. She gave him a warm kiss. "But how am I the hero?" she asked. Before he could answer, a gaggle of young girls demanding hugs surrounded her.

After chatting with as many friends as she could manage, LeeAnn excused herself to head to the washroom. As she passed the kitchen, she peeped through the porthole in the door. Tyler stood, in his official chef's jacket and hat, at the calm centre of a storm of a dozen or so people dishing up a wealth of heavenly dishes. A woman she'd never seen before appeared to be in command of desserts.

Tyler caught her peeping and hustled her away from the door. "No peeking!" He gave her a huge hug. "Congratulations! You're married!"

"What are you doing?"

"Cooking your wedding feast. What else?"

"Did Jesper call you?"

"He did. I told him about the train tracks."

"Ah. That's why he called me a hero."

"Why have you never told him?"

"It happened years ago, long before I met Jesper, and I didn't think it was important."

Tyler nodded. "It was to me. So, when Jesper called…" He paused for a moment. "LeeAnn, I owe you my life. I will be eternally grateful you were there that day." His voice broke, and he strode down the hall. He stopped with his back to her, and leaned against the wall, one hand covering his face.

LeeAnn waited. Her cousin wasn't one for big emotional displays.

He drew a few deep ragged breaths, straightened, adjusted his white hat, and came back. He cupped her shoulders in his hands. "Call it payback in the best way I can… with food from my heart."

She grinned up at him. "In that case, call it even. And thank you!" She pulled him in for another hug. "Now, you need to go back to your kitchen, and I need to go down the hall."

When LeeAnn got back to the foyer, the appetizers were done.

Julia called the whole wedding party forward for group photos. Melody and Hayley snapped with abandon, taking some inside and more outside. They circulated through the crowd for candid shots.

Julia tugged LeeAnn and Jesper to the head of the crowd and opened the auditorium doors with a flourish. LeeAnn took Jesper's arm, and they led their guests into what was now a dining room. This was the only part remaining from Mom's original plan. But the meal was nothing to do with Mom's plans, and everything to do with how well Jesper knew his bride. And, of course, Tyler's incredible cooking made it truly unique—a hearty mix of divine Québécois cuisine and local barbeque specialties, followed by her favourite desserts.

The after-dinner speeches filled LeeAnn with laughter and love, gratitude and a pinch of sorrow. Did anyone anywhere have such wonderful friends?

After the tables had been cleared and moved to make way for dancing, Carlotta ran a flourish on the piano to attract everyone's attention.

Julia stepped onto the dais and raised her arms for silence. "Good evening, everyone."

"Good evening, Julia!" the crowd responded.

"Tonight, we have a special appearance of a trio formed just for this wonderful wedding of two wonderful people, LeeAnn and Jesper." She laughed when hoots and whistles interrupted her. "I'm pretty sure you all know me, Julia Westover, and our world-famous friend Carlotta Pentland…" the crowd added applause to their appreciation, "…but you may not know our guest artist, Marshall Rickerts of the Quâtre Jazz Quartet. Marshall, a friend of Carlotta's, happened to be in town, and he brought his clarinet. So, for this night only, we have the newly minted Stormy Wedding Trio on hand to entertain you all on LeeAnn and Jesper's special day."

LeeAnn peeped over her shoulder at Jesper standing snugly beside her, his arm around her waist. "Did you arrange this?"

He shook his head. "Not a thing. I only called Julia. She put the music together for you."

She frowned. "For us."

"No, my sweet love, for you. Julia, Carlotta, Tyler, Shelby, and Chloe did all this just for you. Because you made a difference in their lives. I only made a few phone calls."

"Jesper," called Julia. "Please lead your beautiful bride onto the floor for your first dance to the dreamy sounds of 'At Last'."

While Carlotta and Marshall played the intro, LeeAnn followed her beaming Jesper to the centre of the floor. Who told Julia they'd been practicing this song in secret? Had she talked to the DJ Norah had hired?

It didn't matter. The Christmas Spirit had obviously been listening to his special elf. Jesper twirled her across the floor, finishing with an elegant dip.

Back in his arms, LeeAnn rose on tiptoe and whispered in his ear. "At last, you are mine and I am yours. Forever."

Thank you for reading *Stormy Wedding*. If you enjoyed these stories and want to help other readers find the same enjoyment, please leave a review or a star rating on your vendor's website or at Goodreads or BookBub.

BOOKS BY JOAN LEACOTT

Clarence Bay Chronicles
Above Scandal
Sight for Sore Eyes
Stormy Wedding

Short Stories
Second Chance Dress
Tollkeeper's Daughter

Meet Joan

Joan Leacott first encountered romantic fiction by sneaking reads of her mom's novels as a teen. She grew so passionate about romance that she now writes her own contemporary multi-generational stories featuring the lives, loves, and scandals of small-town Clarence Bay, Canada. Joan spends her winters in Toronto and her summers on the shores of Georgian Bay near the real-life model for her town Clarence Bay. When she's not writing, Joan loves to practice her patience on her piano; equally entranced by the music and frustrated with fingers that won't cooperate.

Visit Joan's website at wwwJoanLeacott.ca

Or follow Joan on social media https://www.facebook.com/JoanLeacottAuthorPage/